Sue's Voice

Andrew D. Carlson

This is a work of fiction. Names, characters, places and incidents either are the product of the author's imagination or are used fictitiously, and any resemblance to actual persons, living or dead, business establishments, events, or locales is entirely coincidental.

SUE'S VOICE

ISBN: 0692508961
ISBN-13: 978-0692508961

Cast of Characters

<u>Enterprise, Kansas</u>
    Suzanne "Sue" Cook (clone) – cook, Smokey Hill Café
        Violet (clone) – 8 y/o
        Kati (clone) – 7 y/o
    David Hudson – retired
        Zachary (clone) – 13 y/o
        Tyler (clone) – 9 y/o
    Susan Roberts – archivist, DDE Presidential Library
        Karen – 7 y/o
    Petunia Clark – retired
<u>Washington, D.C.</u>
    Ted Stevens – Director, DHS
<u>Tempe, Arizona</u>
    Martha Ross (clone) – barista, Cupz
    Patsy Sharp (clone) – student & barista, Cupz
    Richard Dvorak – student, Arizona State University
<u>Burbank, California</u>
    Donald Jackson (clone) – clerk, DHS
    Denise Jackson – analyst, DHS
        Brandy (clone) – 14 y/o
        Suzanne Theodora (clone baby) – newborn
    Juliana Huffington – analyst, DHS
<u>Spring Green, Wisconsin</u>
    Larry Stone (clone) – farmhand
    Janet Jones (clone) – shop worker, Arena Cheese, Inc.
    Mary MacDonald – retired
<u>Manhattan, Kansas</u>
    Jim Bailey, Ph.D. – Director, Manhattan Laboratory Services
    Sarah Deming – analyst, MLS
    Cindy Gordon – analyst, MLS
    Bruno Jones, Ph.D. – analyst, MLS

Chapter 1 – Su-Su

When Sue woke up, she sighed. She wished that she was wrapped in David's arms. On those days when she was in his arms, she was in heaven. Today wasn't one of those days.

But she quickly shook off her disappointment and focused on the day. Not only was it the anniversary of the clones' release from the base--the clones' Independence Day, it was also another travel day.

As she stood up and stretched, she looked out her window at the mess in her front yard. It was a good mess: the construction equipment and materials to build the addition onto her house. When finished, the boys, Tyler and Zachary, would have rooms in the house, and Violet would get her own room instead of sharing with Kati. Most importantly, David would move in and share the master bedroom. Her chest filled with warmth at the thought. *Every day I'll wake up in his arms.*

Sue walked down the hall to the girls' room.

"Good morning, ladies," she said as she entered.

The two girls were still half-asleep. "It's too early," Kati whined from under her covers. "I don't want to go to school."

"Yeah, Mom, it's too early to wake up for school," Violet added, rolling over and covering up.

"We're not going to school, remember?" Sue cheerfully said to the girls. "We're traveling to Burbank today. We're going to see the baby!"

The girls squealed and jumped out of their beds as if told they'd never have to go to school again. "The baby!" Kati shouted with a big smile.

"We get to see Brandy too!" Violet called out.

"Get dressed in your good clothes. We want to look our best to meet the new baby," Sue told her daughters.

The new baby was Suzanne Theodora Jackson, daughter of Denise and Donald Jackson. Her birth marked the arrival of the next clone generation: the child of a clone.

Sue went back to her room, showered, and put on her best sundress. She wore a sweater over the dress, knowing she could shed it when she got to Southern California.

She went downstairs to make breakfast. When she reached her kitchen, her heart jumped. Sitting quietly at the table, dressed in their traveling clothes were Tyler, Zachary, and David.

"Good morning, Sue," David greeted her.

"Good morning," Sue warmly replied.

"I hope you don't mind that we came over here for breakfast," David said. "I'll help you cook."

"That will be wonderful," Sue replied with a big smile. Any time spent with David was a good time.

"Gentlemen," she asked the boys, "are you ready to go see the baby?"

"Eh… yeah, I guess," Zachary replied.

"Not me," Tyler said. "Babies are stinky."

"But she's Donald and Denise's baby. She's the new clone!" Sue told them.

"But she's still gonna be stinky," Tyler replied, scrunching his nose.

"We'll have a lot of fun in California," Sue said, "I promise."

While cleaning up after breakfast, David looked at his watch and realized time was tight. "C'mon everyone, we only have ten minutes before the van gets here to pick us up. Let's get moving, kids." To Sue, he asked, "Are you ready?"

"Ready to go," she replied with a smile.

The girls came back from downstairs carrying their entertainment for the trip: notebook computers, books and magazines. Sue helped pack them into the overnight bags that were waiting by the front door. When all was packed, Sue turned off the lights and locked the door.

They all walked around the mud and construction debris, past the pool, and around David's house to the driveway that led to the street. Just as they reached the end of the driveway, Petunia, Karen, and Susan joined them from across the street.

"Good morning, Sue," Susan said with a smile.

"Good morning, Susan," Sue happily replied.

Sue, *a.k.a.* Suzanne Cook, was a clone, the copy of Susan Roberts. Sue arrived when Susan touched the pod of "goo". Other than their hair styles--Sue wore her hair long and Susan had short hair, the two were identical.

After greeting each other, the travelers shared conversations while they waited for the van to take them to Abilene. They didn't have to wait long.

The group loaded into the van and rode to the small airport. Waiting on the tarmac was the private jet they all recognized.

They had all rode on the jet two months earlier when Ted escorted all of the clones, their friends, and family to Burbank. There, they joined up with a then-pregnant Denise, Donald, Brandy, and Juliana to meet the Secretary of the Interior and the First Lady. They were recognized for coming up with an official new environmental awareness campaign: "You live on this planet. Clean up after yourself!" And, as Ted promised then, everyone would return when Donald's and Denise's baby was born.

When the van doors opened, the kids rushed out and jumped on the plane. The adults carried the bags and stowed them in the back of the plane. They embarked and greeted Janet, Larry, and Mary who were already on the plane, having been picked up earlier in Wisconsin.

"Happy anniversary!" Sue happily greeted both Janet and Larry.

"And happy anniversary to you!" Janet replied.

"Hey, that's right!" Larry excitedly remembered. "It's been one year since we were released from the base."

"How are you two doing?" Sue asked them.

"Super," Larry replied.

"Didn't we just do this a few weeks ago?" Janet asked.

"We did," Sue replied, smiling.

The mood in the plane was festive. They were

celebrating one milestone and flying to celebrate another.

Ted got on the plane followed by the co-pilot. As the door closed, Ted reminded all, especially the children, to put on their seat belts.

"Thank you, Ted!" Larry called out.

"For what?" Ted asked.

"Our independence," Larry responded.

Sue reminded Ted, "You released us from the base one year ago today, November seventh."

"Thank you," Janet added.

Ted stopped and briefly ran the numbers in his head. "You're right. I honestly didn't remember." He paused again, making sure they were correct. "Then yes, I guess congratulations *are* in order," he said. "Happy anniversary!" He smiled broadly at the clones.

The plane started to roll. When it reached its cruising altitude and the engines throttled back, Mary said, "So Ted and Sue, what do you think about the name of the new baby?"

"I'm honored," Ted replied. "Although, I'm not sure how feminine the name Theodora is."

"You'd be surprised," Mary told him. "There are plenty of famous people named Theodora. Maybe not a lot these days, but historically it's been a very prominent feminine name."

"Then I am even more honored," Ted said.

"I'm honored too," Sue replied.

"Well, it's pretty obvious who our leader is," Janet told Sue. "If they were going to name the baby after anyone, I'd say you were the obvious choice."

The others all nodded in agreement. Sue blushed with pride.

"So Ted," David began, "where are we all

staying? We can't all fit into their condo."

"We have rooms reserved at a local hotel. We'll have plenty of room," Ted told the travelers. "And…" he said loudly, looking at the children to get their attention, "it has a pool."

The kids looked at Ted with a "been there, done that" expression.

"Oh, I forgot," Ted responded. "You already have a pool, so it's no big deal, right?"

"Uh, yeah," Tyler replied. David glared at him for being rude.

"But it's too cold in Kansas to swim now," Ted said, trying to save face. "In California, you can swim all year round."

His comment worked a little. Zachary and Violet both cocked their heads and nodded in agreement. Ted had earned a small point.

The travelers settled in for the short trip to Phoenix to pick up Martha, Patsy, and Richard.

As the plane taxied on the tarmac after landing, Sue took off her belt so she could greet the new group. When the door opened, the three Arizonans got on board. Martha was first and was immediately hugged by her best friend. "Hi Martha!" Sue exclaimed. "It's so good to see you! You look great!"

"Thanks Sue! So do you!" Martha said, smiling. "Wow, we just did this, didn't we? I like these reunions."

"Patsy!" Sue said, as Martha moved back and greeted the others. "How are you? How is school?" She embraced Patsy, too.

"Everything's great, Sue," Patsy said. "All is going well."

"Richard!" Sue continued, even hugging him,

the newest member of the group. "How are you? Are you ready for another exciting trip with us?"

"I wouldn't miss it for anything," he happily told her when they separated.

"Happy anniversary!" Janet told Martha and Patsy. "Today is our anniversary of being released from the base."

"Has it been a year already?" Martha asked.

"What do you mean, 'already'? Has is *only* been a year since we were released? It feels like two years to me," Patsy told the others.

The clones all smiled. They were each grateful for their independence, regardless of how long it felt.

Ted called out that it was time to take off. The travelers all buckled up for the forty-minute ride to Burbank.

When they landed at Bob Hope International, two large vans were waiting at the private hangar to drive them to Denise and Donald's condo. The group deplaned, transferred the bags, divided into two groups, and climbed in. It was a short ride to their destination.

It took a while to get all of the people up the stairs and through the door into the main room of the condo. Once everyone was inside and had found a seat, the party started. They were all together again.

Denise sat in the middle of the room on the sofa, holding the baby. The women and girls flocked around mother and daughter, taking pictures with cameras and cell phones. The men stood back, while Tyler and Zachary went out on the balcony to avoid the whole scene.

"That is the most beautiful baby in the world," Sue told Denise. "She's adorable."

Everyone agreed.

"Yeah," Juliana said, "even with Donald as her father, she turned out to be pretty good looking." She smiled at Donald.

He returned her smile. He was used to Juliana making fun of him.

Ted worked his way into the gaggle of women to look at the baby. "She is beautiful, isn't she?"

"Aw, that's so sweet, Ted," Denise replied. "Thank you."

"Are you getting soft," David asked Ted.

"No," Ted replied. "I honestly think this is one of the most beautiful babies ever. Are you ladies getting a lot of pictures?" He turned back to look at the baby and said, "Suzanne Theodora Jackson."

The room filled with "Aw," followed by silence.

After a few moments, Sue broke the silence, "Can I hold her?"

"Of course," Denise replied. She stood up and carefully transferred her daughter to Sue's arms. All the while, Patsy and Susan took pictures with their cell phones, and Brandy shot video of her sister on her phone.

The crowd of women closed in on Sue and the baby, everyone cooing.

The baby was wide awake and smiling at the people looking in on her. She seemed to study each face, especially Sue's, looking carefully and deliberately.

Martha said, "She really likes you, Sue."

"Yeah, she really does, Sue." Denise added.

The baby smiled.

"It's like she knows she's named after you, Sue," Patsy said.

The women agreed and captured the moment with pictures. Brandy pushed in to get video of Sue with the baby.

Suzanne shifted in Sue's arms, and turned her head slightly for a better view of who was holding her. Above the quiet clicking of cameras, the baby made bubbles and gurgled.

"Oh, look," David said, "the baby's making noises."

"How cute is that?" Brandy added, continuing to shoot video clips.

Suzanne responded by gurgling more, not just random, but seemingly intentional.

"She's making more noises. It's like she's talking to us," Ted said with a smile, thinking it was cute.

Mary, Petunia, and Susan, the experienced mothers in the crowd, all looked at each other with concern. *Babies don't gurgle like that at this age.*

The baby continued to make bubbles and noises while smiling at Sue.

Brandy said, "She really likes you, Sue."

The baby babbled, "Su-Su."

ANDREW D. CARLSON

Chapter 2 - Let's Just Hope

The room fell quiet. No cameras clicked and no one spoke. Everyone just stared at the baby that was smiling and gurgling in Sue's arms.

After several long moments, Mary finally broke the silence and asked the group, "Did that baby just talk?"

"I heard it," Petunia said.

"She said 'Su-Su', I think," Juliana replied.

"That's not right," Susan said aloud. "There's no way a baby can talk this early in life."

The group stood or sat in silence, trying to understand what had happened. Even the children knew that the baby shouldn't be talking.

Denise reached out and nervously held Juliana's hand since Donald was too far away. The others remained silent, looking at each other.

Ted put his hand on his chin and stared at the floor, thinking. He broke the silence when he said, "Last summer, when I went to the lab, they were breeding mice, children of the original cloned mice."

The adults all looked to Ted to hear his thoughts.

He looked up and scanned the faces around him, especially Denise's face, before continuing, "The children of the cloned mice learned very quickly. They were able to do amazing things. They learned the mazes faster than normal mice, faster even than their clone parents. They figured out the boxes and tubes faster, and helped each other get food. They learned quickly and better. Perhaps Suzanne, here, is just like the other children of clones."

The others looked at him with continued interest, not speaking.

"The life cycle of a lab mouse is so fast compared to a human," Ted said, "they probably didn't see any developmental acceleration. Or they couldn't recognize it if it did occur."

"What are you saying, Ted?" Denise asked with concern.

"I don't know. I'm thinking out loud here. But if the next generation of mice from a cloned parent can do really amazing things, why shouldn't the next generation of humans? Why shouldn't Suzanne be as amazing?"

"The difference," Mary jumped in and clarified, "is that we know how human babies develop and can observe them. What the lab couldn't see with the mice, we can see happening to Suzanne."

"So talking at seven weeks is normal for the children of clones?" Denise asked, stunned and shocked.

"I don't know what's normal. There's only one baby. Suzanne is it," Ted said. "Now that this happened, and based on what we know from the mice,

I don't think we should be surprised by anything that she'll do in the future."

"This is so not right," Juliana said out loud. "No offense," she told Denise, squeezing her hand more tightly, "but this is one unusual baby."

Denise sat silently, thinking about her baby.

Brandy broke the silence by saying, "Well, at least we got it on video." She thumbed and swiped her cell phone. "We wouldn't want to miss it."

Jokingly, David turned to Donald and said, "You'll have to keep a video camera on her at all times, twenty-four seven."

"Wait a minute," Ted said urgently. "Brandy, did you film Suzanne talking? Did you get it on video?"

"Yeah. Why?"

"What did you do with it?" Ted asked intensely.

"I... uh... posted it on YouTube," Brandy replied nervously. "I post lots of pictures and videos."

"Delete it immediately," Ted ordered.

"Why?"

"There cannot be a video of a seven-week-old baby talking on the internet," Ted insisted.

The others raised their eyebrows, raised their shoulders, and turned up the palms of their hands.

"What if people in the government see the video, especially those nuts on the Committee? They'd go crazy and know she's not normal. They'll have a sign that the 'aliens', as they refer to you all, really are alien."

"But those old codgers don't watch YouTube," David countered. "Hell, I don't even watch YouTube and I'm way more in touch than they are."

"And anyone who saw it probably would think it was so weird that it had to be a doctored video,"

Richard said. "You know, like a photo-shopped video."

"Delete it," Ted firmly told Brandy.

Everyone watched as Brandy fumbled on her phone to find the video. When she did, her eyes widened in shock.

"What?" Denise asked.

"There've been ten views already. It's only been a few minutes," Brandy told the others.

"Delete it," Ted sternly repeated.

Brandy poked the screen of her phone, and then nodded at Ted to confirm it was done.

"Let's just hope no one in DHS saw it," he said.

Chapter 3 - slijmerij

Patsy tried to ease the tension in the room by changing the subject. She announced, "Sue reminded us on the plane that today is our one-year anniversary. One year ago, Ted let us start our new lives."

"Can you believe that it's already been a whole year?" Janet asked. "It seems like only a couple months. We were just together a few weeks ago, and it felt then like we had just been released."

"Time flies, don't ya know," Larry added.

"I agree," Martha said. "It seems like yesterday when I started working at Cupz. It's been a whole year, but I'm still learning."

"Speaking of learning," Juliana said, "what about you, Patsy? You spent this year studying hard to get your GED. Did time fly for you too?"

"It's hard to say," Patsy replied. "It does seem like a short time, but I was so busy studying and working, that it feels like I did two years worth of things."

"What about you, Brandy?" Sue asked.

"I don't know," Brandy said, considering all that had happened the past year. "I guess it feels right. We went right to school and then I had a busy summer, and now I'm back in school."

"Wait, Patsy called out. "You're in high school now, aren't you?" she asked. "How's that going?"

"Pretty good," Brandy replied. "A lot of my friends were really nervous to start at high school, but it didn't seem like that big of a deal for me."

"How are your grades?" Sue asked.

Denise started to open her mouth to boast and brag about her daughter, but Brandy shot her a look. "I'm getting good grades," Brandy modestly replied.

"That's really good," Sue said. "The girls and boys are all at the top of their classes. When David and I met with the teachers, they all had good things to say. I'd say we have some pretty smart kids, don't we?" Sue asked the group, scanning the room to see everyone's responses.

There was definite agreement among all in the condo. Even Suzanne gave a little gurgle.

Ted reminded the group, "Don't forget that we have lunch reservations at Harry's. It's the only place that could handle twenty people."

"You mean twenty-one," Denise said, pointing at Suzanne.

"Correct," Ted said, smiling. "There are now twenty-one of us. And if we're going to get all twenty-one of us to the restaurant on time, we better get going. Denise, what help do you need? I'm sure one or two of the visitors can assist. I assume you don't mind Sue holding the baby while you get organized."

"I don't think I could pry her out of Sue's arms if I had to," Denise said with a smile. Her daughter filled her with warmth, and watching Sue hold her namesake was precious. "I'll just pack a bag for her and get the car seat and then we'll be ready."

The group finally got moving after ten minutes. Donald, Denise, Brandy, and the baby rode in their car, and they led the vans to Harry's.

The lunch was organized chaos given the size of their party, but they managed to get seated, order food, and eat in just under two hours. After lunch, the group loaded back into their vehicles and returned to the condo.

"Does the baby need to sleep?" Mary asked Denise, once inside.

"No, she slept a bit at the restaurant and in the car on the way back," Denise said. "Sure, she'll need a good nap in a little bit, but she's okay for now."

The group dispersed; the children went to the balcony, the adults stayed in the main room.

Brandy sat in the corner with her phone. She checked her Instagram account, and commented on her friends' latest pictures. When she had commented on those that deserved it, she instinctively opened YouTube to see what was trending. She didn't find anything interesting, and her thoughts pulled her back to the video of her sister. She was amazed at how many people saw it on YouTube in the short time that it was posted. She thought about why Ted was so insistent. *What's the big deal? I mean, I guess it is a little freaky that the baby talked. But it was cute. But I guess that's not why it's bad. The baby babbling wasn't normal. Yeah, okay, if it went viral, it would be all over the internet, and Ted probably wouldn't like that. But there's no way one of my videos would ever go viral.*

She clicked to open Twitter. She looked at her

connections and saw a new follower: @eline913. She checked out the new follower's profile: Eline van der Bach, from the Netherlands. *Eline... That's a pretty name. She looks pretty too. But why is someone from the Netherlands following me? Oh well, a follower is a follower.* She followed Eline back, as is good Twitter practice.

She scrolled through the recent tweets only half-interested. As she scrolled, she was pinged with a notification, a new direct message. *That's odd.* She clicked and found the message. *It's from that Eline girl.* She read it:

> @bjack1313 I saw your video on
> YT. Is the baby your sister?

Brandy quickly shut off her phone in a panic. *Oh my god! She saw the video! And she found me! What do I do?* She looked around the room until her eyes fell upon Sue. *Sue! I can trust Sue. How do I talk to her without it looking weird?*

Brandy stood up and slowly walked over to where Sue was sitting. "Hey Sue, can I ask you a question?"

"Sure," Sue happily replied.

"Can I ask it private?"

"Sure," Sue happily said again, not suspecting anything.

Denise, on the other hand, was suspicious. "Why in private?" she asked.

"It's a surprise, Mom," Brandy replied.

"With Sue?" Denise asked, skeptically.

"Yeah, with Sue," Brandy said tersely. She fumbled for an answer that would placate. "She's a real cook, Mom, and that's all I'll say."

Her mother nodded and Sue stood. Brandy led Sue to her bedroom. "This is a pretty room," Sue said as she entered.

Brandy closed the door and guided Sue to the far wall of the room. Her face was full of fear. "I need to talk to you in private. You can't tell anyone."

Seeing Brandy's face, Sue quietly asked, "What is it?"

"Do you promise to keep this a secret forever?"

"Yes, Brandy, I do," Sue replied seriously without a smile or her usual excitement.

"I got a message on Twitter," Brandy began. "It's from a girl in the Netherlands. She saw the YouTube video. She's asking if the baby is my sister. What do I do?"

"She's from the Netherlands? That's in Europe, right?"

"Yes. What do I do?"

"Why are you so scared?"

"I don't know. I can't explain it. But don't you think it's weird that a girl in the Netherlands saw my video, which was only posted for a few minutes, finds me on Twitter, and then asks if the girl was my sister? She didn't even see me in the video. She only saw Suzanne."

"I don't know much about Twitter and that kind of stuff, but yeah, I guess it seems a little weird, like a coincidence."

"What do we do?" Brandy asked nervously.

"What can it hurt to respond and say yes?"

"She saw the baby talking. Remember, this is a *newborn baby*. What if she reports us?"

"To who?"

"I don't know!" Brandy said, getting agitated.

Sue put her hand on Brandy's arm and quietly told her everything was okay. "Why don't you at least respond and say hello. That can't be bad, can it?"

"I guess not," Brandy said hesitantly. She took out her phone, found the direct message, and replied.

> @eline913 Hi from California. Yes
> that's my little sister.

"There."

"Okay, good," Sue said.

"We'll see if she replies," Brandy said.

"Let me know when she does, okay? I'm here for you, Brandy," Sue told her.

"Thanks."

Sue turned to leave the room, but as she did, the cell phone pinged. Brandy swiped her phone. "She replied!" Brandy called out in a whisper.

"What did she say?" Sue asked.

Brandy looked at the message, her head tilted and her face scrunched in confusion. She held out the phone to Sue to show her the message.

> @bjack1313 Are you made from
> the... I don't know the english, in
> dutch we say slijm or slijmerij

"What does that mean?" Sue asked.

Brandy shook her head.

"Does your phone translate?"

"I can google it and see," Brandy replied. She typed the first word into Google and waited. "Ew, it means mucus. Does that make any sense?"

"What else do those words mean?"

Brandy typed in the other word. "Google doesn't find it... Oh wait, there's a translator link." She tapped her phone and her eyes immediately went wide with shock.

"What?" Sue asked eagerly.

"It translates as 'goo'."

Chapter 4 - Reply

Sue was as stunned as Brandy. "She asked if we were from 'goo'. Does that mean that she knows about our goo?" Sue asked. "Does she know about our substance and where we came from?"

"What if she came from the goo, too? What if she's a clone like us?" Brandy asked.

"I don't know," Sue replied. She looked down at the floor, darting her eyes back and forth. She was too surprised to think.

"We gotta tell Ted," Brandy said. "He'll know what to do."

"No," Sue immediately told her. "We can't."

"Why not?"

"Ted will make you stop talking to her. He'll try to make things disappear so the government won't know about her."

"Is that bad?" Brandy asked.

"It is if we want to find out more. If there are more of us clones around the world, I want to know. I want to learn more about them. I want to know if they have messages. Maybe they have the same messages as us." Sue stood silently in Brandy's room, thinking of what to do.

The door of the bedroom opened up and Denise poked her head inside. "Is everything okay in here?" she asked.

"Yeah," Brandy said. "We're just talking."

"Okay, I was just checking. You've been in here for a while."

Brandy took a breath and sighed. "We're fine, Mom," she replied, trying not to give any attitude.

"Okay, I'll leave you two. Keep talking," Denise said as she turned and closed the door.

"We'll talk later," Sue quietly told Brandy. "Until then, don't tell anyone."

"Okay."

The two opened the door and re-entered the main room. The room was quiet. Denise and Juliana both held their fingers up to their lips, silently telling Sue and Brandy the baby was sleeping.

Ted whispered to the adults, "I think it's time for us to leave and check into the hotel. That'll give the Jacksons a little space for a while."

The others nodded and they all stood up. David retrieved the younger kids from the balcony and ushered them outside the door where they met the rest of the group in the hallway.

"We'll give you a couple hours to breathe," Ted whispered to Denise and Donald. "We reserved the little conference room at the hotel. We'll have dinner catered in. The food won't arrive until seven o'clock, so take your time, relax, and come on over with that little baby when you're ready."

Denise and Donald thanked Ted.

Before they could close the door, Brandy asked. "Can I go with them?"

"Sure, that's fine," Denise quickly replied. "It's ok, right Ted? You have room in the vans, right?"

"We've got plenty of room," Ted said. "C'mon."

Brandy joined the others leaving the condo. They climbed in the vans and drove to the hotel. It wasn't a long drive.

When they pulled up to the entrance and all got out, Ted gave instructions to the adults, and then went inside to check in.

While Ted was away, Brandy approached Sue and asked, "Will we have time to talk later?"

David, who was standing alongside Sue, looked at Brandy with confusion. Sue saw David's expression and tried to cover for Brandy. "Girl things," she told him. "And baby things," she added. She smiled at David and then at Brandy.

Ted returned and handed out keys to each of the rooms. He told everyone to get their luggage and follow him. He led the way carrying his overnight bag.

As they walked to the rooms, they passed the inner courtyard containing the heated pool. The children begged to go swimming. Sue, David, and Susan agreed, but told them they had to wait as long as it would take to get to the rooms and unpack.

When they reached the adjoining rooms for Sue and David, Brandy offered to keep an eye on the kids while they swam. David thanked her, and Sue offered to join her, smiling.

Brandy went outside and waited by the pool. She checked Twitter; no new message from @eline913.

Sue brought the kids out and they immediately

jumped in the pool. Sue took a seat next to Brandy and started talking. "I've been thinking," she said, "Ted knows about us and knows that we're human, right?"

"Yeah."

"But he doesn't know about anyone else in the world, right?"

"I guess not," Brandy replied.

"But if he did know about other people, he'd know that they're human, right?" Sue asked.

"I guess so. He'd probably assume they are, since he tested us and we're human," Brandy said. "So if they came from the same goo, they're human too."

"So there's nothing to fear from these other people, right?" Sue asked.

"Not for Ted, but what about the rest of the government? They probably want to know about the other people," Brandy said.

"But the people are in other countries. Our government can only be concerned with Americans."

"So we don't have to be so careful," Brandy concluded. "We can tell Ted and he won't care, because they're not in this country." They both sat and thought for a moment about their logic. "Then why did he care so much about the video?" Brandy finally asked. "Why did he want me to delete it?"

"Maybe because Suzanne is a new clone, you know, someone that people don't know is a clone, and since she's almost talking, other people would recognize her as being weird, unusual."

"So he must think that finding new clones in other places is bad. But why? Why are new clones so bad?" Brandy asked.

Sue shook her head. She had no answer.

"What if we ask Mary or David, or Mom?"

Brandy proposed. "Maybe they'll know why Ted would think new clones are bad."

"We can't tell them about the new girl in the Netherlands," Sue said. "They'll tell Ted."

"Yeah, I guess you're right."

The two sat silently and watched the kids play in the pool. After several minutes, Brandy asked Sue, "What should we do? We never replied to Eline. We never told her we're from the goo. Should I reply?"

"Yes," Sue said. "You should definitely reply."

When Sue took the kids up to the rooms to change into dry clothes, Brandy found the conference room and found a seat off to the side. She took out her phone and composed a new direct message:

> @eline913 Yes we are from the goo
> or slijmerij. How did you know?

The Wisconsin group and the Arizona folks were already sitting in the room and talking with Susan and Petunia when David and Sue brought the kids down a short while later. Denise and Donald arrived with Suzanne, and Juliana brought up the rear with the stroller. The women flocked to the baby. The men sat and talked.

Dinner was brought in as scheduled at seven o'clock. Sue helped serve the kids and then the adults helped themselves.

"I hope you don't find me to be too sentimental," Mary said aloud to the whole group while everyone ate, "but I'd like for each of us to share our thoughts with each other now that we've been relocated for one whole year. Or, for some of you, the non-clones, how your lives changed significantly one year ago." She looked at David with a smile when she said the latter.

"For instance," Mary continued, "I am thankful to be retired. I only have to care for myself. Yes, I helped Janet and Larry adjust to life in Wisconsin when we first moved there. None of us expected the winter to be *that* cold." She shivered, remembering the temperatures. "And, yes, I taught Larry how to drive, but he and Janet don't need any help anymore. They're on their own. And I enjoy being with them, but it's not a responsibility. Today, I'm just a friend. I couldn't be happier."

A chorus of "Aw" filled the room.

"And we love to have Mary around as a friend," Janet added. "Don't we, Larry?"

"You betchya."

"And we love to be out on our own," Janet continued. "I love my job and meeting new people. And Spring Green is so nice. The leaves this fall were spectacular, weren't they, Lar?"

"You betchya."

"I know we're supposed to have been born and grown up in Wisconsin, but I'm not sure I'm ready for the snow and the freezing cold temperatures again." Janet shook her head and gave a little shudder. "It's already gettin' cold there now, don't ya think, Lar?"

"You betchya!" the rest of the group replied. They all had a good laugh. Even Larry laughed along with the others.

"I know we're only young'uns, since we were born just last year, but I feel like an old person," Larry told the others. "I'm not sure if that makes any sense, but I feel like I'm a regular guy livin' a regular life in Wisconsin."

"I know what you mean," Patsy said. "Yeah, we're all only one year old, but I feel like I'm a college student. I study, I drink coffee, I work when I can, I got a boyfriend, and I got a roommate." She smiled at both Richard and Martha. "It's weird, but we all fit in where we live. It's like the nature or nurture debate."

"You're right" Richard jumped in. "You all are clones of your other people, but yet, you don't act like them. You all adapted to your new homes and your new situations. And you don't act like you've only been here for a year. You act like you've been here for as long as you appear."

"That's weird," Patsy said. "I look like a college student, and we're surrounded by college students, so I act like a college student."

"Not me," Martha told Patsy. "I hang out with the college students, but I act like I'm older."

"That's because people treat you like you're older," Richard said.

"Yeah, but I bet Martha feels and acts a lot younger than her other person." Pasty looked to Ted for confirmation.

So did everyone else.

"Hey," Ted replied with his hands up, "I don't keep track of your other people and compare you to them. I don't know how Martha's person acts or thinks."

"Look at the two Sues," David said. The others looked to him, and then to Susan and Sue. "They're clones. They have the same DNA. They even look the same, except for their hair. 'Nature' is the same for

27

them," David pointed out. "But do they act the same? No way. Susan is quiet and relaxed while Sue is... well, Sue. So 'nurture' makes those two very different."

"Interesting," Ted said aloud. "I never thought about it that way. I guess I never thought that your surroundings can not only affect your behavior, but also determine it." He and the group thought about it for a minute.

"Would Patsy behave the same as Sue if she had two daughters and worked in a restaurant?" Martha asked.

"I don't know," Pasty replied. "But that's a really interesting question, Martha. That would have been cool to find out. Of course, we can't erase our memories and start back at the base anymore, can we?" Pasty asked the others.

All the clones shook their heads defiantly and said, "No." They all agreed that starting over at the base was not what any of them wanted.

Three people from the caterer came into the room. They removed the entrees and brought in coffee for the group. "Sit down," Ted instructed Martha and Juliana with a smile. He was half joking, half serious. "We can serve ourselves coffee tonight," he added.

Serving coffee was Martha's self-declared assignment when they were all at the base. Juliana had been recruited by Martha to be assistant barista.

Martha smiled at Ted, appreciating his comment. Juliana snapped her fingers, feigning disappointment, even though she, too, smiled at his joke.

"Well, I for one love my new life," Sue told the others as they sat and sipped. "I could not imagine doing anything different than what I do now. I don't know what I would do if I didn't work at the café and have the kids."

"Don't forget David," Juliana reminded Sue with a big grin.

"Of course I won't forget David," Sue said. "He's the best thing that happened since I moved." She took his hand and held it.

"I know I'm not a clone," Susan said, "although, I guess I did create one... Anyways, I know that life on our street, even the whole town, has changed since Sue and the kids arrived. It's like there's a whole new energy. Karen has new friends, and we do almost everything together, so I can't imagine what life would be like without them."

"I agree," Petunia added. "Life in Enterprise is very different, but very good."

The others in the room smiled and said, "Aw."

"I agree with that," Juliana said with a smile. "Life with these three... now four, has been a total wild ride. Not that Donald is a crazy man or anything, but because of how normal the Jacksons are. I mean, look at them... Denise marries a clone and they adopt another one. And then a year later, they have one of their own. And all the while, he goes to work, Brandy goes to school, and Denise takes care of the baby. That's like totally normal and totally weird."

"Um, how?" Brandy asked. "It's totally normal. That's what we are."

"Sure, you are all normal, and no one could tell where you actually came from, but think about where you came from!" Juliana excitedly told the others. "Just a year ago, eleven people appeared from blobs of goo because other people touched it. You all showed up knowing nothing, with no memories, and now a year later, it's like nothing weird happened." She looked around the room at the blank looks. "Apparently I'm the only one who finds this a little freaky."

"We're just normal people, Aunt Julie," Brandy told her. "And the reason why it's not weird is because we have people like you to help us fit in and learn and become normal."

"That's sweet, kid," Juliana said, "but I still thinks it's weird… in a big picture kind of way."

"Yeah, it's weird," Denise spoke up. "I mean, look at me. I married a clone. And I adopted one. And I gave birth to one!" Her eyes went wide. She seemed to surprise herself. "What was I thinking?" She paused a moment, and then continued, "But yet, it's not weird. You're a normal person, Donald. And I love you. You're normal, Brandy, and I love you. And I love Suzanne," she said looking at her sleeping baby. "Who cares where you came from? You're here and we're all glad you are."

"And I'm glad I am here," Donald said, looking at Denise. "And I'm so happy to be part of your life… our life. I don't even think about where I came from, I just think about where we're going."

"You betchya!" Larry called out. Everyone in the room laughed.

"Hey, we forgot Ted," Sue told the others. "What about you, Ted? What do you think after a whole year of us living on our own?"

"Well, it's been one hell of a ride," Ted replied smiling. "This adventure has been exciting, challenging, and heartwarming. It has been a pleasure to experience it with you all."

"Here, here!" David called out, raising his coffee cup.

"And here's to the future and watching you all for many years to come," Ted said.

Awhile later, the catering staff came back in the room and cleaned up. It gave the group a chance to stand up, stretch their legs, and break off into smaller conversations.

Brandy approached Sue and pulled her aside, away from the others. "She didn't respond. I sent Eline a direct message, but she hasn't responded. The way she responded so quickly before, I thought she would have by now."

"Maybe she's eating dinner or out with friends," Sue said. "She'll be back later and will reply then."

"Oh Wait. Duh!" Brandy said quietly but emphatically, shaking her head. "How could I be so stupid? She's in the Netherlands. That's in Europe. They're on a totally different time zone than us."

"Which time zone? What time is it there?"

"Let me look it up." Brandy swiped and tapped her phone. "Netherlands... they're nine hours away from California. It's six in the morning there."

"No wonder she didn't respond. She's still sleeping. We'll see her response in the morning, our time," Sue said. She smiled at Brandy and gave her a pat on the arm.

Sue turned to look for her daughters and found them lying on the floor, asleep, along with Karen. Tyler was asleep as well. Only Zachary was still awake, playing a video game on the system Ted arranged for the kids. Sue walked up to David, tapped him on the shoulder, and then pointed to the children. "I think it's time to go upstairs and go to bed. It's been a long day for them."

"They're still on Central time," David said.

"Can you get the girls? Susan and Petunia can help." David motioned to Susan, who got the hint. The Kansas adults said goodnight to the others, collected their children, and went upstairs.

Having also woke on Central time, Janet, Larry, and Mary agreed that it was time to get ready for bed, so they followed a few minutes later.

Martha, Patsy, and Richard stayed and talked with Ted and the California group for a while, and then decided to turn in. Ted said goodnight and followed the Arizona bunch upstairs.

With no one else remaining in the conference room, Donald carried the baby to the car, while Denise, Brandy, and Juliana followed. They drove in silence to the condo. It had been a busy day. They said goodnight and separated, Juliana to her apartment, and the Jacksons to theirs.

Denise and Donald did baby-maintenance things: changing, feeding, and singing lullabies. Brandy went to her room, flopped on her bed, and tapped her phone, scanning her Instagram and Twitter accounts.

Around 11:00, Brandy received a response from Eline:

> @bjack1313 You are from the goo too! I saw the video of your sister talking. I just knew. There are others from the goo like us. Let us talk.

Chapter 5 - You're It

"C'mon, Mom," Brandy urgently told Denise. "We gotta get to the hotel. We'll be late."

"There's no rush," Denise said. "There's no set time to meet."

"You seem nervous, kid," Donald noted. "What's up?"

"Nothing. I just want to see everyone."

"Well, the baby's not ready yet, so it'll be a few minutes," Denise said. She and Donald were casually collecting diapers, clothes, bottles, and Suzanne's favorite toys.

Brandy stood in the middle of the room with her arms folded, tapping the floor. She sighed for greater effect.

"It's a Saturday, B," Donald said. "We don't have anywhere to be."

"Um, at the hotel," Brandy quickly replied.

"They'll be there all day," Denise said. "What's got into you? Why are you so anxious to go?"

Realizing she might be pushing too much,

Brandy dialed her attitude back a notch. "I just want to go see and talk to the others, that's all." She dropped her arms and sat on the couch. She looked relaxed on the outside, but on the inside she was a mess. She had to get to the hotel to tell Sue what Eline had written.

Finally, all of the baby's supplies, as well as the baby, were ready to go. "Okay, let's go," Brandy said, leading her mother to the door.

"We can't go until Juliana gets here, sweetie."

"Oh!" Brandy said, tipping her head back and looking at the ceiling in frustration. "Well when is she gonna get here?" she snapped.

She didn't have to wait long. The intercom buzzed and Denise let Juliana in. As soon as Juliana opened the door, Brandy guided everyone out.

"She's a little antsy to get to the hotel," Denise informed Juliana. "We better get going."

They all piled in the car and set out for the hotel. "So what's the deal, sis?" Juliana asked Brandy.

"Nuthin'. I just want to get to the hotel."

"Yeah, but you're like a dog that has to go outside to pee. You aren't normally like this," Juliana told her.

"I know, but I just want to talk to the others," Brandy responded, looking down.

Juliana left it at that. They rode in silence, except for the gurgling of Suzanne.

As soon as they reached the hotel, Brandy gently pushed Juliana out of the back seat and ran past her, into the hotel and into the meeting room. She found Sue talking with Martha and Patsy, all of them sipping coffee.

Brandy approached Sue and from behind and asked, "Can we talk?"

Sue held up a finger to pause the conversation with Martha and Patsy, and turned to talk to Brandy. "Did you get a response?" she whispered.

Brandy nodded excitedly.

Sue excused herself and walked with Brandy to the corner, leaving Martha and Patsy confused. "Okay, what did the message say?" Sue quietly asked Brandy.

"She said that she was from the goo too," Brandy whispered. Her eyes were wide and she fidgeted with her hands. "And she said 'Let's talk.' She saw the video of Suzanne talking and knew she was from the goo. And she also said there were others. What should we do?"

"We definitely talk to her," Sue said quietly, with determination. "If there are other clones in the world, we should find out about them. We should find out about their lives. We should see if they've got messages too."

"How should I respond? What should I say?" Brandy nervously looked at Sue.

"I don't know. Let's think about it for a little bit. We have to say just the right things."

Sue and Brandy stood in silence for a while trying to come up with a response for Eline. But they couldn't. Nothing came to mind.

"Let's go talk with the others for awhile," Sue suggested calmly. "Something will come to us."

"Okay," Brandy reluctantly agreed.

The two casually mixed in with the others who were gathered around Suzanne, the focal point of conversation.

It was Patsy's turn to hold the baby. As she looked into Suzanne's eyes and watched her squirm and gurgle, Patsy smiled from ear to ear.

"Now don't go getting any ideas," Richard sternly told Patsy. The others laughed, but not Richard. He was serious.

"Don't worry, Richard," Pasty said. "I have no interest in having a baby." She looked over and smiled at Richard. She added, "At least not right now."

"Oh great," Richard replied, rolling his eyes.

David nudged him, leaned in, and quietly said, "Join the club." He and Richard chuckled.

The women continued to gush and coo over the baby. They babbled and spoke baby talk while smiling at Suzanne. The men stood back and watched, but none of them were going to get in the mix, not even Donald. He loved his baby, but he was not about to displace a dozen women and girls to look at or hold his child. He knew he'd have plenty of time when the weekend ended.

Throughout the session, the women repeatedly said the baby's name as they gushed over her. Suzanne responded by gurgling and babbling. As before, the baby caught everyone off guard by saying, "Su-Su."

Although the people in the room were not as stunned as when the baby first talked, they were still surprised. As she held the baby in her arms, Patsy shook her head and said, "That is just not right."

The others agreed.

"Denise," Ted spoke up, "I wonder if you'd consider something."

Denise looked at Ted and shook her head. "I don't think I like this," she replied.

"It's not bad, I promise," Ted told her. "It's a matter of scientific curiosity."

"Now I know I don't like it."

"Hear me out," Ted said. He pointed to the

baby and said, "Your baby can talk. That's not normal. There's no debate. She's also the daughter of a clone, a man who appeared on Earth as an exact copy of another man who touched a substance that landed on the handle of a dumpster behind a grocery store in Florida. That's not normal. Do we all agree?"

Everyone silently nodded.

"So don't you think it's wise to find out as much about this baby as possible?"

"I don't know," Denise replied.

"We tested the clones," Ted continued. "Their DNA matches their other people. We know that. But we also know that there's something else there. They get messages." He looked around at the clones and said, "You can read and write in an alien message. We know that mice cloned from the very same substance display remarkable behavior. And the offspring of the cloned mice are equally amazing, maybe more." He stopped to gauge the response from Denise and Donald.

They considered Ted's argument. Donald seemed sold. Denise was not. "I don't know if I want Suzanne tested," Denise said. "What will they do, put her in a maze to find the cheese?"

Ted chuckled and said, "No, nothing like that." He shook his head and waved his hands. "I think that a DNA test is all that we'd do. We'll see what her DNA looks like compared to you and to Donald."

"What if they find something? What if she has a genetic defect or something like that?" Denise asked, very concerned with the proposal. "I don't want to know anything about that. I couldn't live with that."

"The probability of Suzanne having a genetic disorder is very slim, not because she's immune or special, but because the probability of anyone having a genetic disorder is very low."

Denise was not convinced. She continued to scowl at Ted. The others opted to stay out of the discussion. It was between Ted and Denise.

Before it could continue, the conversation was halted when lunch was delivered. Tension in the room broke. The kids were allowed to get food first, followed by the others. Denise took the opportunity to feed Suzanne. And Brandy talked with Sue.

Ted stepped out of the room and made a call to Dr. Jim Bailey from Manhattan Laboratory Services. "Jim, it's Ted. ... Yes, I realize it's Saturday and I'm sorry to disturb you. But, once again, I'm with the clones. We're all together in Burbank, visiting the new baby. ... Yes, Donald and Denise's daughter. You will not believe what just happened. ... Yes, that's exactly what happened! She said 'Su-Su' out loud for all to hear. She said it twice."

Ted listened to the laboratory Director for a few moments, and then continued, "Here's what I think we should do. I think we should do a much more detailed DNA sequencing of the baby. There has got to be something there. There is no earthly way that a seven-week-old baby can talk. There has to be something in that baby's DNA. And there's probably something in the clones' DNA. We just didn't look hard enough last time. So what kind of test can we do besides the fingerprint?"

He listened as Jim gave options. "Shotgun sequencing? That's complete sequencing, not just a fingerprint, correct? ... And if there's something in the clones' DNA, we'll see it? ... Okay, good. I have to get the mother's permission before we do anything, so I'll call you later. ... Thank you, Jim. And again, I'm sorry to disturb you on a Saturday. Goodbye, Jim."

Ted went back into the meeting room and served himself a plate of food. He joined the adults who were sitting in the middle of the room.

The children had a table set up for them off to the side. Brandy sat with them at the table, not to be part of their group, but to be away from the adults so she could send a message to Eline:

> @eline913 what do you mean by
> others? how many? where are they
> from? there are 11 of us cloned
> from the goo here in the U.S.

Brandy looked over to Sue and made eye contact. She nodded at Sue and briefly held up her phone, indicating that she had sent a response.

The group had pleasant conversation while eating, and after the meal was cleaned, up, the caterer brought in the coffee.

"What's on tap for the rest of the afternoon?" David asked Ted. "Are we doing anything in particular?"

"Well, we're not really able to do much with the new baby. I don't think Denise wants to go mobile with Suzanne yet," Ted replied. Denise shook her head, confirming Ted's assumption. "And it's very hard to get reservations at restaurants or other places." He looked around the room for agreement. No one voiced any objection. "I thought we'd be able to entertain ourselves while we're all together. We haven't had much trouble with that in the past."

"True," Sue said. "We can usually talk about

anything between us." She smiled at the adults and said, "In fact, let's start a new conversation." Sue turned to Ted and asked, "How did you find all of us, Ted?"

"That's an odd conversation," Ted replied with a skeptical look. "Why do you ask?"

"Well, I know that you came to get me at Susan's house a few days after I arrived from the goo. But how did you find out about me? Did Spike call you?"

"Yes, you know that," Ted replied, looking more confused.

"What about the others? How did you find out about them?"

"Local law enforcement notified DHS. Why are you asking? What are you getting at?" His eyebrows raised and furled in suspicion.

"I'm wondering if you found all of the clones."

Ted dropped his stern expression and replaced it with doubt. *Does she know something? Does she know of other clones?*

The others also looked at Sue with concern.

Sue recognized the dramatic change in mood. She said, "I don't know anything, Ted. I'm just wondering if we're the only clones. I mean, don't you think it's weird that the goo came to Earth and the eleven of us are the only people that were cloned?"

"You eleven aren't the only things that were cloned," Ted told the group. He looked around the room before continuing. All eyes were on him. "There were many animals that were cloned by the goo. We started noticing numbers of primates go up in zoos across the U.S. And a bear cub was actually cloned, too. And David here," he pointed to David, "had a few too many gophers in his yard because of the goo. So you all were not the only things cloned."

He stopped to wait for a response. No one said a word. They all waited for him to continue. He sighed and said, "The goo arrived all at once. All of the discoveries associated with it were made within a six to eight-week period. We relied on reports from the law enforcement community to discover the significant events."

"You mean us, correct?" Sue asked.

"Yes."

"But what if a law enforcement person didn't report another clone?" Sue challenged Ted.

"How could they not?" Ted asked, raising his hands and shoulders. "A new person arrives on the planet and local LEOs don't think it's a big deal? That's absolutely not possible. They would have reported it."

"But what if no one discovered the new person?" Patsy asked.

"Impossible," Ted replied.

"Why do you say that?" Sue asked.

"The new person had to be cloned by another person, so there had to be at least one person in the area. And, unless they lived in the middle of nowhere, there must have been more people around."

"But it is possible," Patsy said.

"My other person didn't notice me," Donald reminded Ted.

"Okay, I suppose it is possible," Ted said, a little irritated, "but new people had no clothes, no memory, and no skills. If a clone was left alone in the middle of nowhere, they would have died. They would have no way to get food or protect themselves."

He paused for a moment, the suspicious look returning to his face, and turned to Sue. "Why did you think to ask that question?" He knew something wasn't quite right. That was too odd of a question to ask, even for Sue.

"I don't know," she replied. "I guess I just wonder if we're the only clones." She looked around to the other clones.

"You're it," Ted said firmly. "I'm sure of it."

A long silence filled the room. Ted's irritation radiated across the room, shutting down any further discussion on the matter.

The kids moved off to the side to play video game, Brandy found a corner to text her friends, and the adults awkwardly searched for a new topic of conversation.

The baby started to squirm and cry. The women moved in to assist while the men broke off in side conversations.

Ted took the opportunity of the diversion to leave the room and walk outside to stand in the warm California air. He paced in the parking lot.

What does Sue know? Does she know something? Or was her question just curiosity? And did we find all of the clones? ... Of course we did. There is no way that a new person could go unseen and unreported. There is just no way. ... But what if we missed one? It would have died, right? A clone would have no skills to survive on their own. And if someone found them, they would have reported it. ... No, we did not miss anyone. Sue's just curious. She doesn't know anything.

Shaking his head of the thoughts, Ted took a deep breath and went back to the meeting room to join the party.

The women were taking turns cooing over the

baby whom Martha was proudly holding. Donald held a dirty diaper at arm's length, looking for a place to dispose of it.

Ted slid into a conversation with the men and the rest of the afternoon passed with no more tension.

As the sun set and dinner was brought in to the room, the adults sat together. Patsy started the conversation. "So Sue," she began, "you've got a new house, a new pool, and now a new addition to your new house. So, what's next, a new car?"

The other clones looked at each other smiling. They were all jealous of Sue. She could get whatever she wanted from Ted.

"You all know why we have a pool," Sue replied seriously. "We have four kids, five if you count Karen, and it gets hot in Kansas in the summer."

"What about the addition to your house?" Patsy asked.

Sue blushed and replied, "Well… that's needed because the kids need their own room, eventually."

"And?" Juliana asked, jumping in.

"And that's it," Sue replied. But there was more, and the others knew it.

"Nothing else, huh? Just some extra rooms for later, huh?" Juliana asked with a big grin, hoping Sue would keep talking. She was rewarded.

"Well… there might be a wedding some day," Sue replied, blushing even more.

Juliana cackled with delight. Patsy and the other women squealed with surprise and happiness.

Even the men were surprised to hear Sue's news. Donald leaned over to David and said, "Welcome to the club."

David rolled his eyes and sarcastically said,

"Thanks."

"Are you ready?" Ted asked David.

"No, but I don't think that will stop her," he replied, pointing his thumb to Sue.

"Good luck," Richard told David.

"Thanks."

Coffee was brought in after dinner. Denise left the room to change and feed Suzanne. When she returned with her happy, gurgling baby, she handed her off to the next woman in line: Janet.

"So Sue," Denise said as she sat down, "Tell us about this wedding you're planning."

"Well, I don't have much to tell," Sue admitted, blushing. "I haven't really talked about this yet with David."

All eyes moved to David to see his response.

"Hey," he replied, holding up his hands, "this is the first I've heard of it."

Sue hurried over to David and put her hands on his shoulder. She leaned in and kissed him on the cheek. "True," she said aloud, "but it's still a good idea, right?"

David chuckled and shook his head. "No place like a room full of people to float the idea of marriage," he said.

The others in the room laughed. Sue did too.

"I think it's sweet," Patsy said. "It's another example of how we're all living our new lives."

"So Richard, care to join me and Donald?" David asked. We might as well get you hitched at the same time."

Richard blushed, but didn't respond.

David noticed. He smiled, and asked him, "You're really thinking about it, aren't you?"

Richard just shrugged.

"Patsy, is this first you've heard of this?" David asked, expecting her to be as surprised as he was.

Patsy blushed. "Well…" she said quietly and slowly. "We have talked about it a little," she said, looking at Richard.

Juliana cackled again at potential nuptials among the group. The others in the room started laughing with pleasure.

"Our wedding was small and quiet," Denise said aloud. "But Sue and Patsy's weddings better be big parties."

"What about a double wedding?" Juliana proposed. "Patsy and Sue can both get married. They can do it in the summer in Kansas. And we can all fly there, another reunion!"

"That sounds great!" Martha replied. "We'll get it catered and have a DJ."

"You betchya," Larry called out.

Everyone laughed.

Ted raised his hands and said, "Before you all go planning a wedding for next summer, let's let Sue discuss this with David first. And Patsy and Richard might also need a little time. I'm not quite sure the men are ready yet."

When she and her family arrived back at the condo, Brandy went to her room, changed her clothes and climbed into bed. She swiped and tapped her phone, checking social media.

She was almost asleep when her phone pinged: a Twitter notification. She opened the message.

> @bjack1313 There are 4 in
> Netherlands, 2 in France, 1 in
> Belgium, 2 in UK, 2 in Sweden.
> Those are the people I know.

Brandy sat up straight in bed. "Wow," she said to herself. "Ted would flip out if he knew about this."

"What's that, sweetie?" Denise said from outside her door.

"Uh... nothing. I was just laughing about someone's tweet," she replied. "Goodnight."

"Goodnight, dear," Denise said.

Brandy thought about Eline's message. *How did she find out about the nine other people? And how did the video of my sister talking make Eline know that she and I were cloned from the goo?* She typed:

> @eline913 How did you find the
> others? We were all in a camp until
> the U.S. government let us go. We
> now live normal lives.

Having exceeded her character limit, she typed an additional message:

> @eline913 How did you know my
> sister was a clone? She is the baby of
> a clone. The rest of us were cloned
> from other people by the goo.

She sat and stared at her phone, waiting for a reply. It came right away.

@bjack1313 I was detained with 2 others. We heard of others in Europe. I remembered how many. I have been looking for them.

And:

@bjack1313 The other 2 here had a child. She was born 10 weeks ago. She also talked. That is not normal. So I guessed your sister was like us.

And:

@bjack1313 What is your email? Can we send email instead of Twitter?

Brandy replied and gave Eline her email address. She patiently waited for an email message. Again, she didn't have to wait long.

Hello Brandy,
  I'm glad you gave me your email address. It will be easier to communicate.
  When I appeared, I was taken by the police. I was detained with two other people from my country, a man and a woman. I listened carefully to the police. And I also talked to the police men.
  They were nice and told me some things. They didn't tell me other things. I was able to learn there were others in Europe who were copied by touching the goo.

You said the people in the U.S. were cloned. Does that mean you are genetic copies? Has DNA been tested?

Do you know the others in the U.S.? Were you detained together or separate?

There is so much information I want to know. I hope you will still exchange email messages with me. And I hope my English is good. I hope you can understand my writing.

Your new friend, Eline

"Wow," Brandy whispered.

Dear Eline,

Your English is very good. I can understand you very well.

There are 11 clones in the U.S. And yes, we are clones. We were tested for our DNA fingerprints. We are copies of the people who touched the goo.

All 11 of us were put together at a military base. Some people wanted to keep us there forever. But the government man in charge of us proved that we were normal humans and he let us go. He helped us find homes and families and jobs.

We are all friends. In fact, we are all together right now at my home in California. They are visiting my sister.

You said the other two clones in your country had a baby. And it talked too? Did the adults get married? Do they live together? And where do you live?

I was adopted by a government worker at the

base. She is really nice and a great mom. But she's not my real mom since I have no real actual mother. She married another clone. They fell in love. It was sweet. They had the baby. So the baby is not really my sister, but she basically is. Does that make sense?

Tell me about you.

Your friend, Brandy

Chapter 6 - You Have My Word

The vans arrived at Donald and Denise's condominium on Sunday morning.

"Brandy," Denise called to her daughter, "it's time to get up. The others are here from the hotel." She listened for signs of life, but did not hear any. She opened Brandy's bedroom door to find her still asleep. Denise quietly walked over to the bed and sat down. She softly said, "It's time to wake up, sweetie. You need to get dressed to see the others."

Brandy groaned and covered her head with her blanket. Denise patiently waited. Finally, a voice from under the covers asked, "What time is it?"

"It's nine o'clock. What time did you go to bed last night?"

"I don't know," the sleepy voice replied. "It was around midnight, I think, maybe later."

"What were you doing?" Denise asked.

"I don't know, just texting and stuff."

"Well, take your time," Denise told her, "but not too much time."

"Okay," Brandy said still groggy.

Denise left Brandy's room and joined the guests. Donald had already lost control of Suzanne to her namesake. Sue cooed and babbled at the baby who gurgled in return.

The other women gathered around and added to the cooing. They made faces at the baby, smiled at her, held her little hands, and talked to her. And, as before, receiving all the attention she was getting, the baby replied, "Su-Su."

"Denise," Ted said, putting his hands up in self-defense, "I know you don't like the idea of testing the baby, but I think we should. There has got to be an explanation for this behavior."

"Do you expect to find a talking-baby gene?" Denise asked, irritated at Ted.

"No. You know that is not what we'd be looking for." He paused before continuing his proposal. "Don't you wonder what's going on? Why does this one baby talk at seven weeks?"

"It's the baby of a clone," Donald replied in his wife's defense. "You know it. We all know it. We don't have to test for it."

"We thought you all were totally normal last year," Ted said. "Then we found out you can read and write a new language. And now we have a baby that is talking at seven weeks old. Maybe you all aren't as normal as we thought."

"But the DNA test proved we were normal," Patsy said. "We matched our other people."

"That was a good DNA fingerprint test," Ted replied. "But it's not very detailed. What I'm proposing is a full sequencing of the baby's DNA, and probably yours too, Donald and Denise."

"What?" Denise shot back.

"We need to compare the baby to its parents," Ted calmly responded. "It's not much use if we don't have anything to compare to."

"What does this do for us?" Sue asked Ted. "Last time we tested our DNA, it was to get us off the base and into our new lives. This DNA testing won't do us any good."

Ted sat and thought about Sue's argument. "You're right," he finally concluded. "I can't see the use of the results other than pure scientific research." He looked to the others to see their responses.

The clones were not happy. Neither was Denise.

"*Confidential* scientific research," Ted added. There was no change in anyone's expression, so he continued, "You eleven clones are advanced humans. We know that. We know that you have better metabolism. We know that you can better control your body temperatures in extreme conditions. We know that you are the future of humanity. We should document it. History will want to know about you and your children. And maybe someday scientists can use what we find for the good of everyone."

The whole group sat and thought about what Ted had told them, including Brandy who had quietly joined the group. They all knew that the clones were advanced humans. It was difficult for the clones to argue against documenting their DNA.

David asked Ted, "Where will you put this information? Who will know about it? Where will it be stored? Will your committee *friends* see it?"

"Yeah, what if the committee finds the results?" Juliana asked. "Won't that be bad? They might use it against the clones somehow."

Ted stared at the floor thinking. He hadn't yet thought that far. After a few moments, he looked up and said, "Only the lab will know. And I'm sure we can keep that number down to only the director and his group leaders. I trust them implicitly."

"Can *we* trust them?" Denise asked.

"Definitely," Ted replied. "Remember the fingerprint testing?" The others nodded. "I'll have the lab director give me all the notebooks. I'll be the only one who has the data. And no, I will not share it." He looked around at the others in the room. "If you can't trust me, who can you trust? I'm sure that someday, in the future, I will divulge all I know. Until then, the results will be safe with me and remain confidential."

The room was silent. No one was arguing with Ted. They were all trying to find the flaw in the plan.

"You're all here. We have Donald and Denise and their baby. We even have Susan to compare to Sue."

"Wait a minute," Susan blurted out.

Ted gestured his hands toward the floor to calm Susan. "It won't have as much value of we don't test a clone against the original," he said. "And you're the only original person we can approach. The others should be left alone."

Susan scowled silently at Ted.

"It will be confidential. And no one will be looking through your DNA, Susan. They'll be looking through Sue's DNA. They're just comparing what's there to what's not there."

Ted could still detect resistance in the room. "What if I get a conference call with the lab director? If you hear him tell you that all will be confidential, will you agree?"

Susan and Denise both raised their eyebrows and nodded reluctantly.

Ted pulled out his phone, put it on speaker and dialed Jim Bailey's cell phone.

"Jim, it's Ted," he brightly said.

"It's Sunday, Ted. Don't you ever stop working?" Jim asked.

"Not really," Ted replied honestly. "Listen, you're on speaker-phone right now. I'm here in California with the clones and their families, the whole group. I've suggested to them that we test the baby, the mother, and the father using complete DNA sequencing. We also have Sue and her original person, Susan. You'll be looking only for sequence differences between clones and non-clones. Is that correct? You won't be looking for anything else, right?"

"Yes, that's correct," Jim replied. "The test would look for DNA differences between the clones and the non-clones. We would not identify specific genes or search through common sequences. We'd just look for the differences."

"And how will you control the information?" Ted asked Jim.

"I assume that we'll do it the same as last time," Jim said. "We'll destroy all the DNA samples, and all the data will be in specific notebooks that we'll give to you when we're finished."

"What about any electronic data?" David asked out loud for Jim to hear.

"We can delete the files after we transfer the information into the notebooks."

"And the people? What about the security of your analysts?" David asked.

"They do confidential testing all the time," Jim replied. "They actually sign confidentiality agreements when they accept employment at the lab. Everything is confidential. I've never had a security breach yet. Besides, only the group leaders will know where the samples came from or why we're doing the testing. The analysts won't know anything. They'll just be analyzing samples A and B. So there is even more control."

Ted let the people in the room reflect on what they'd been told. Seeing no resistance, he said aloud, "Thank you for your time, Jim. I'll talk to you soon."

"Okay, Ted," Jim replied.

Ted hung up his phone.

"I don't like it, Ted," Denise said. "I don't want my DNA, my whole DNA sequence, on file somewhere. I guess I can understand about Donald and Sue, even Suzanne, although I don't like it. So why me? And why Susan?"

"You know it is not relevant without the non-clones. And you're Suzanne's mother. We definitely need your sequence." Turning to the others, he added, "You too, Susan. We need your non-clone sequence to compare to Sue's clone sequence. Without it, Sue's data is practically meaningless."

"I just don't like what might happen to my DNA sequence," Denise replied.

"Me too," Susan added. "What would happen if my sequence falls into the wrong hands? What could someone do with it?"

"I don't think anything bad could come of it," Ted replied. "Yes, it's a lot of information, but I don't see what could be done with it. Someone could look at your sequence, but they can't use the information for anything. They can only read the sequence differences. The lab is looking only for differences."

Mary sat up straight in the middle of the group and said, "I think Ted is right. I know you don't like it, Susan and Denise, but we really need the data."

"Et tu, Mary?" Denise asked.

"Yes," Mary replied. She scanned the faces in the room and continued, "If you clones really are the future of humanity, people are going to want to know why and how. If we don't do the sequencing now, under our terms and conditions, someone else in the future might do it under their terms and conditions. If we do it now, we'll avoid doing it in the future. And maybe, by doing it now, you all can remain anonymous, especially the children."

The group sat quietly and considered Mary's comments. After a few long moments, heads started to nod. The clones agreed that testing under their own control would definitely be better than under someone else's.

"We're relying on you, Ted, to keep this confidential," Sue told him. "No one wants Susan hurt by this. No one wants Denise hurt by this."

Ted looked to each of the clones, to Susan, and to Denise. He had no expression on his face, other than plain honesty. "You have my word that I will be in control of the data." Seeing no immediate objection among the faces, he added, "You trusted me before. You can trust me now."

Ted scanned the room twice over to look for resistance. There was none. "I need to go to the pharmacy. Juliana, can you be my guide in Burbank?"

"Yeah, I'll go," she flatly replied. Ted silently motioned to Juliana, and the two of them left the condominium.

No one in the room was happy or excited. No one was upset any longer, but Susan and Denise were still skeptical.

Eventually, quiet conversation filled the room as they all waited for Ted and Juliana to return.

Brandy approached Sue and motioned for her to step away from the group. When they reached the kitchen, Brandy whispered to Sue, "I got an email message from Eline. We stopped using Twitter and started emailing. She told me more about herself."

"What did you find out?" Sue asked quietly.

"There are, like, ten clones in Europe. At least that's how many she knows of. And two clones in her country had a baby, just like Mom and Don, and she could talk too. That's how Eline knew that Suzanne was a clone."

"Wow," Sue replied. "We're not alone." She stood quietly, staring at the floor, thinking about what she had learned in the past two days. "Did she send any more emails?" Sue asked.

"Not any today," Brandy replied. "I guess she's busy during the day, so I'll get one later today, maybe." She paused and then asked Sue, "What should we ask Eline? What do we want to know?"

"We want to know as much as possible," Sue replied eagerly. "We need to find out all we can. We need to know how many clones there are and where they are."

"Why?"

"The clones are like a family. We need to know where all of our relatives are. We need to know how many people are in our family."

"Are you saying we should meet them all?"

"I don't know," Sue replied honestly, shaking her head. "I don't know what we should do or what we can do. But I think we need to at least know how many clones there are on Earth."

"Do you want me to send you the emails from Eline? Or do you want me to just tell you about them?"

"Whatever you think is best," Sue replied. "You know way more about email and texting stuff than I do." She paused for a moment, thinking hard, her eyes darting back and forth, and then rhetorically asked Brandy, "I wonder if she can read and write our language."

"Should we send her a letter, you know, a paper letter?"

"I think so."

"But I don't have her address."

"We'll need to get it," Sue said.

"But I can't write a letter by myself," Brandy reminded Sue. "You and the other kids have to do it from Kansas."

"Yes."

"Won't David find out what we're doing? He'll tell Mom."

"He might," Sue replied. "Let me think about that for a while. But in the mean time, you and I will send emails to each other, and you can email Eline. Let's see how much we can find out."

"If Eline asks about us, should I tell her all I know?"

"I think so," Sue replied. "If she tells us everything about them, we should tell her everything about us."

"Do you think they have a committee in

Europe, like they have here in the U.S.?" Brandy asked.

"I don't know. You could ask Eline."

"Do you think she'll get in trouble if someone finds out about her talking to us? We'd probably be in trouble if Ted's committee found out about Eline."

"Are you sure?" Sue asked. "She's not in the United States, so the committee shouldn't care who else is a clone, as long as they aren't in the U.S."

"I don't think they trust us," Brandy said. "If they knew there were more clones on the planet, don't you think they'd be more scared or angry?"

"I don't know, Brandy. But you're right, we need to be quiet about this. Don't let your Mom or Donald know. I won't let David know. Then Ted won't find out."

"Okay."

Denise walked over to the kitchen and said, "You two have been talking for a while. Anything interesting?"

"No, just boring stuff, Mom," Brandy replied with a smile.

"Young women stuff," Sue said with a confident nod. Denise looked at her skeptically, to which Sue responded, "Hey, I'm not that old. I know how a young lady thinks."

Ted and Juliana interrupted the conversations in the room when they returned with supplies.

"Okay," Ted said, "who's first?"

Sue, being the closest to Ted, volunteered. She sat on a chair in the kitchen while ted rubbed the inside of her cheek with a swab. After collecting the sample, Ted placed the swab in a new, sterile tube and sealed it with the cap. He wrote "K2" on the tube and added "(c)" for clone.

"Next," Ted said to Susan. Susan took a seat on the stool and Ted repeated the process. He labeled the tube "K1".

He continued with Donald and Denise, labeling their samples as "C2(c)" and "C1", respectively. "Okay, now for Su-Su," Ted said.

Denise held the baby while Ted managed to swab the inside of her cheek despite her constant gurgling and babbling. He placed the swab in the sample tube. He labeled the tube "C3(c2)".

"Okay, that's it. We have the samples," Ted said. "And don't worry, the information will not get out, I promise."

The test subjects nodded.

Mary changed the subject by asking, "Ted, what time does the plane depart?"

"Wheels up at one o'clock," he replied.

"That's only two hours from now," Mary said. "Knowing this group, we should start to say goodbye soon."

Martha and Juliana served one more round of coffee and talked with each person as they made their rounds. Conversations continued for an hour before Ted announced it was time to go.

David rounded up the Kansas kids while the others started saying goodbye. Everyone knew that an opportunity would soon arise for the group to get back together, so the departure was a happy event, everyone looking to the future.

Ted led the way out of the condominium, followed by David, Susan, and the kids. Petunia, the Wisconsin group, and the Arizona bunch followed after.

Sue lagged behind the others, giving herself

time to talk to Brandy. The two walked out into the hall and closed the door behind them.

"Don't forget to email me and Eline," Sue said.

"And don't forget to write a letter to Eline," Brandy told her. "I'll get her mailing address and send it to you."

"It's a deal," Sue replied. "This is exciting," she added. "We have a chance to meet other clones from around the world. I hope we can actually see them in person."

Brandy nodded and smiled. "Goodbye, Sue. I'll see you soon."

The two hugged, and then Sue scurried to catch up to the rest of the travelers.

Chapter 7 - No, We Didn't

The vans arrived at the airport and pulled up to the waiting airplane. The travelers all got out. Again, the kids ran onto the plane while the adults helped load the luggage. When everyone was buckled in, the plane took off.

Forty minutes later, they landed in Phoenix. The group got out and stood on the tarmac to say goodbye.

"Keep studying hard," Sue told Patsy. To Richard, she said "It was great to see you again."

They hugged and moved down the line to continue saying goodbye.

Sue told Martha, "I'm so glad we got to see each other again, and so soon."

"Me too, Sue. And you had better keep us updated on your wedding plans," Martha said.

Sue blushed. "Maybe I rushed that a little," she replied. "Then again, it is a good idea." She smiled.

"I hope I can be a bridesmaid," Martha told her.

"Of course you will be! Don't be silly."

"Thanks. See you soon, Sue. Be good."

"I will," Sue replied. She reached out for Martha and they hugged.

When the goodbyes were finished, Ted instructed the others onto the plane and they took off for Kansas. The remaining travelers talked among themselves the entire time during the flight.

When the plane landed in Abilene, everyone got off to repeat the goodbyes. When complete, Ted announced that Janet, Larry, and Mary were to get back on board to fly to Wisconsin.

"Wait! Why aren't you going?" Sue asked.

"I'm staying here overnight so I can drop off the samples in Manhattan tomorrow."

"Oh yeah," Sue said.

"I assume I can bunk with one of you in a spare bedroom?" he asked, looking to Sue and then to David.

They both replied, "Of course."

The Kansas folks walked to the waiting van and waved goodbye to those on the plane.

It was a short drive to Enterprise. The van pulled into David's driveway as the sun began to set.

"I don't suppose we could have a group dinner, with all of us," Ted suggested.

"Sure, what's one more person?" David replied.

"That's gotta be expensive," Ted said, "feeding nine people every night?"

"We don't go all out, and we all pitch in, so it's no big deal," David told Ted.

Susan added, "I can't keep Karen away from the other children, so it makes sense for me to join them."

"And I enjoy the company," Petunia said, "so I tag along."

"What should I bring?" Ted asked.

"Tonight, you can bring you," Sue replied.

Susan took Karen home to unpack. Petunia walked across the street with them and peeled off to her house. David took the boys inside his house. Ted followed Sue and the girls to her house.

Ted sat in the family room and checked his email while waiting for the others to congregate.

When the meal was ready, David called to the kids. Like well-trained wait staff at a restaurant, the boys pulled the folding table and chairs from the closet and set them up for the children. The girls brought in the silverware for all and laid them out on the adult table, as well as the kid table. David and Sue dished the meal onto plates and poured drinks.

Ted was amazed at the sight. He turned to Petunia and asked, "Is this normal? Or is this just a show for guests?"

"Oh no," Petunia replied. "David and Sue have it planned like this every night. It's a well-orchestrated unit."

"Wow," Ted said. Petunia and Susan laughed.

After dinner, the maneuvers to clean up continued. The kids dutifully brought their dishes into the kitchen, scraped off the few scraps, and placed them into the dishwasher. Sue and David followed the kids and within minutes, the dishwasher was running and the kitchen was clean.

"Amazing," Ted said shaking his head.

The boys watched TV while the girls went upstairs. The adults sat in the kitchen and talked. "I don't mean to re-open the subject," Susan said, "but I'm still nervous about the additional DNA testing. I don't like that my DNA is being tested again, and in such depth."

Trying to re-assure Susan, Ted calmly said, "Has anything happened to the original tests that we performed last year? Have those results leaked?"

"No."

"And I still have those notebooks. I did not let the Committee keep them. They're locked in my personal safe at home." He paused before continuing.

Susan nodded.

"And you saw how I labeled the tubes. The only thing that could get anyone close to you is the letter K. I don't think you can be tracked down from that."

"True, but if someone connects the samples to the clones, to Sue, it will then be obvious who the other sample belonged to."

"Yes, but the lab personnel don't know who you are. The director is the only one who knows who you are, by first name only, not by full name or address."

"I'm still nervous."

"I promise you that I will keep your identity confidential," Ted said.

Susan nodded, but did not smile at Ted.

"Do you think the DNA will tell us anything?" Sue asked Ted. "If there are differences between Susan and me, or between Denise and Donald and Suzanne, what will that mean?"

"I'm afraid I can't answer that from a scientific perspective. I guess, since the human genome has been mapped, they might be able to see which genes are different. Maybe they can pinpoint the genes that give you the evolutionary advantages."

"Can they use it to screen for other clones?"

Sue asked.

Ted scowled as he looked at Sue. "What do you mean? We know who the clones are. We're looking to see what makes you different."

"But what if you haven't found all the clones? What if there are more clones in the U.S., or maybe in Canada, or Mexico, or even Europe? Can the test be used to search for clones?"

Ted sat frozen in his chair, staring at Sue. The scowl remained on his face.

Sue patiently waited for his response.

The others waited for Ted's response.

Ted continued staring at Sue. Finally he said, "I don't know what you know Sue. Maybe you don't know anything. But if there are other clones out there, and notice I used the word *if*, I assume the test might be able to show that a clone is a clone. But we have no reports from any other country that other clones were found."

"Did you report us to other countries?" Sue asked.

Again, Ted froze. Only his eyes moved, darting from side to side as he faced Sue. "No," he said slowly. "We didn't."

Sue raised her eyebrows and shrugged, silently asking Ted if it was possible that other clones existed.

"I get your point, Sue," he replied. "I suppose it might be possible that other clones exist. But I highly doubt it."

David offered to make coffee. The others nodded, accepting the offer.

While David played the part of barista, Petunia asked Ted, "How is the 'Clean Up the Planet' campaign going? Is it taking hold?"

I talked to the Secretary of the Interior last week. He said the First Lady is continuing her tours and is well received. The press is spreading the word, so I think it's on its way. We'll have to wait and see just how effective it is. He was optimistic."

"Fantastic!" Petunia replied.

"You all should be very proud," Ted said, looking specifically at Sue.

Sue blushed and smiled with pride.

David served the coffee, and the adults sipped while the sound of the TV drifted into the room, along with the boys laughing. The girls could be heard giggling upstairs

The adults made small-talk about the kids and their grades in school, Sue's cuisine at the café, and Susan's job at the presidential library.

Although they woke up in California, two hours behind Kansas, the excitement of seeing everyone over the weekend, combined with the air travel, eventually caught up to everyone. Petunia yawned, followed by Susan. The laughing and giggling from the kids died down. David walked into the family room to find the boys asleep on the floor.

"I guess I better get Karen home," Susan said.

"Where can I find a room to crash?" Ted asked.

"You can crash in my spare room," David told him. "I might need a hand carrying the boys."

"Fair enough," Ted replied.

The women stood up and went upstairs to check on the girls. Petunia and Susan soon came down with a very groggy Karen. They left Sue's house followed by the men and boys.

Ted helped David get the boys into their beds before saying goodnight to David and going to his room.

He changed into his sleeping clothes and climbed into bed. But he didn't fall asleep right away.

What does Sue know? Why did she ask about other clones? Does she know something? Or is she just that smart? It does make sense that there are other clones out there, I guess. I mean, the pods didn't just land in the central part of the United States. They had to land all over the planet, right? If so, there may be many more clones out there. But were they found? Are there really other clones out there?

Chapter 8 - Find Out

Ted woke up when David and the boys did. He tried to stay out of the way as they got ready for school. The sun had barely risen before Violet and Kati arrived at the house. Sue was already at work at the café.

Ted sipped his coffee while David ushered the kids out the door. He waited in silence until David returned.

"Whew," David said. "I don't know if I'll ever get used to that. It's so hard to get them moving in the winter," David said. Then he chuckled, adding, "They're up at the crack of dawn in the summer, ready to go outside, but in the winter... nooo."

"Well at least they'll all be under one roof soon," Ted said.

"That'll be easier for the girls, but that's a few more showers that will be needed under the one roof."

"Looks like you and Sue will need to do some coordinating," Ted replied.

"Yep."

"So David," Ted began, "what did you make of

69

Sue's comments?"

"About other clones around the world?"

"Yeah."

"I don't know. I guess it makes sense that clones exist elsewhere, unless the goo only landed here in the U.S."

"Which is unlikely," Ted replied.

"Yeah."

"Has Sue ever talked to you about this before?"

"No, never."

"So this weekend was the first time you heard her talk about this?" Ted asked.

"Yeah." David sat for a minute. "What does that mean?"

"I'm not sure. But something happened this weekend while we were in California. There has to be a connection."

"Okay, but what?" David asked.

"I don't know yet. But there has to be some reason why it came up this weekend." Ted scratched his chin for a few moments before telling David, "Let me know if you learn anything."

"Will do."

"Okay," Ted said as he stood. "Now I have to take a shower and get over to Manhattan with the samples, if you will excuse me."

"Be my guest."

After showering and getting dressed, Ted sat with David in the front room of the house, having one last cup of coffee.

"Should Susan and Denise be nervous?" David asked Ted.

"About the DNA testing?" he confirmed. "No, not those two. It's the clones that will be most exposed. If there is a difference and we find it, there will be markers to identify the clones. It's the same gamble we faced a year ago. If the DNA fingerprints had matched, great, they're human. If they hadn't, there was a way to identify the clones, a reason to keep them isolated."

"Then why do the additional testing?"

"We need to know about the clones. We have an obligation to know what it is about them that makes them so smart and why they develop and learn so quickly. It's important, especially when they might be the key to survival on this planet."

"But you're going to sit on the data, keep it confidential, right?"

"For now," Ted replied. "I have to. It's not time to introduce the clones to the world as the future of humanity. But someday it will be the right time."

"I'll leave that to you, Ted. But until that day, we're all trusting that you and the lab can keep the test results confidential."

"I'm not worried about me or the lab," Ted replied confidently. He took his last sip, stood, and said, "Time to go. It's been a fun couple of days, David. I look forward to the next visit. Say 'Hi' to Sue for me when she comes home this evening."

"I will," David said as the two shook hands.

When he pulled into the parking lot of Manhattan Laboratory Services, Ted got out, carrying his briefcase, samples inside.

Jim greeted him at the front entrance and showed him into the conference room. Already seated in the room were Jim's group leaders: Sarah, Cindy, and Bruno. "Hi Ted," they called out.

"What brings you all the way out here?" Sarah asked.

"Good morning," Ted replied. "And I'll tell you why in a few minutes."

Jim and Ted took seats with the others. Ted began, "We all know that what I bring you stays confidential. And your lab techs haven't breached that confidentiality yet, but I have to repeat that what I'm about to tell you stays *highly* confidential." He looked to the others in the room. "Are we good?"

They all silently nodded.

"Good," he replied. "I have to say it, even though you know it. The details I'm about to tell you cannot be shared with anyone who works here. No specifics will be shared. Always use code. Are we in agreement?"

The others nodded. "Ted," Jim replied, "we're covered. We screen all of our techs. And my group leads can be trusted."

"Okay," Ted said. "I have some cheek swab samples for you to analyze. I need a complete DNA analysis. I need to look for needles in a haystack."

"Didn't we do this already?" Cindy asked.

"We just did a quick fingerprint last time," Bruno corrected her.

"Correct," Jim said. "This time we'll be doing complete sequencing."

"I assume we'll be comparing the results to the human genome?" Bruno asked.

"Nope, to each other," Ted said. "I can't give you any more details other than there are two sets of samples. The samples in each set should be compared to each other."

"Okay," Jim said aloud. "The sequencing should not take long to complete. The tough part will be the analysis, the comparison of samples to each other."

"How long will it take?" Ted asked.

"That depends on the number of analysts we use," Jim replied. "We can put ten people on each sample, or we can put one person on each."

"I don't need results tomorrow," Ted said. "I need them in a few months. And I don't need a lot of people looking at these. The fewer, the better."

"We should be able to do that," Jim answered. "We'll hire a few temp workers for the analysis. Maybe we can get a couple students from the universities in the area."

"Okay, sounds good," Ted said. He reached in his briefcase and pulled out the six tubes. "Here they are."

Cindy and Sarah took the samples from Ted. "What do C and K mean? Is this all the information we have to work with?" Cindy asked.

"That's it," Ted replied. "I coded the samples and only I know the coding. That's all you get."

"K must mean Kansas, for the clone that lives here in Kansas," Sarah said.

Ted squirmed in his seat. "Uh, not necessarily," he replied. Then, turning to Jim, he said, "Only you four can see these codes I just gave you. Everyone else only sees random numbers that you generate. Only you will know how the random numbers relate to the codes I give you, okay?"

"You got it, Ted."

"And don't confuse them," Ted warned. If you

do, all of this will be wasted effort."

"We got it covered, Ted," Jim replied. "I promise."

"Okay, then that's it. That's all I have. I'll wait for the results. And remember, all electronic files will be deleted after the data are transferred to notebooks. And I get the notebooks when you're done. No other copies remain here at MLS, right?"

"Yes, Ted. We know the drill."

"Okay, Jim, thank you. Cindy, Sarah, Bruno, that will be all. Can you please excuse me and Jim?"

Jim looked surprised, but then nodded at his team leaders. They shrugged, accepting the request, and then walked out of the room.

"There's something else," Ted quietly told Jim.

"Okay, what?" Jim asked.

"What's the probability there are more clones out there?"

"Out where?"

"On the planet."

"Oh," Jim said. He thought for a moment, and then clarified, "Human clones?"

"Yes, human."

"Um... pretty high, I guess," Jim said, "unless the pods of the substance arrived only in the U.S., which is not likely. It's logical that they landed all around the Earth when they fell from the sky. A lot of them probably degraded quickly in the sun and the heat. And those that landed at the poles froze. But those that landed in temperate climates should have been capable of producing clones."

"It was September when they arrived here. It was relatively cool in the Northern Hemisphere." Ted said.

"But it was also spring in the Southern Hemisphere," Jim pointed out.

"So there could be clones all over the world," Ted said to himself, out loud.

"There could be," Jim replied flatly. Both men knew the consequences.

"But wait," Jim called out. "You would have known about them. Your department would have known about other new people in other countries, right?"

"We didn't tell anyone about our clones," Ted replied. "Why would other countries tell us about their clones?"

Jim sat silently.

"What we find out about our clones will impact all of the clones around the world, if there are any others," Ted said. "We know of our eleven clones, well, now twelve. But there have to be others out there. What if there are a hundred clones, or a thousand?" Ted asked. "Twelve are bad enough, but a thousand? If the public ever found out…"

The two men sat quietly for several moments. Finally, Jim said, "Ted, I don't know what to tell you."

Ted replied, "Find out what makes the clones unique and don't tell anyone. The lives of more than just twelve people are in jeopardy."

Chapter 9 - How Cool Is That?

Brandy was too busy during the school week to focus on sending an email message to Eline. But on Saturday, she lay in bed, pretending to sleep, and tapped a message to her new friend.

Hi Eline,

I'm sorry I didn't write for so long. I have school and soccer during the week.

I have a clone friend here in the U.S. Her name is Sue. She is older than I am. She arrived at the same time as me, but her other person is older than my person was. So she is a mother and has a job.

We want to send you a letter written by hand, not on a computer. Can we send you a letter? Do you have a mail address where we can send you this paper letter?

Also, what do you do? How old was your other person? Are you in school? What do you like to do?

I'm 14 years old. I like to study science and math. My friends and I are all smart. I like to play soccer too. I think you call it football. I'm not the best player on the team, but I'm pretty good. I like being in California. The weather is nice all of the year.

Please write back and tell me what you like to do. Thanks!

Your friend, Brandy

Brandy got out of bed and took a shower before joining her parents and sister in the family room.

Juliana had come over, as she normally did. "Hey, sis," Juliana said to Brandy. "How's it going?"

"Not bad, Auntie. I got an A on my math test yesterday, and I scored a goal in my game."

"Nice! You rock!" Juliana replied.

"Thanks," Brandy said, smiling broadly.

"Let's see if you can score any points on me," Donald said, waving the controller for the video game.

"Madden NFL?" Brandy confirmed. "I'll kick your butt, as usual," she proudly replied.

While Donald and Brandy played the game, Juliana helped Denise with the baby and made lunch.

After lunch, Brandy went to her room to get her English book to read for class. While there, her phone vibrated. "Eline replied!" she said quietly. She sat on the bed and read the message.

Hello Brandy,

I included my postal code at the bottom of the message. I look forward to reading the letter.

I am also age 14. I am in my third year of secondary school. You call it high school, except we go from age 12 to 18. I also play football, or soccer as you call it. I am a forward. I like science and math as do you.

My family is nice. My assigned mother and father knew about my appearance. They are actually related to the family of my other person, as you call her. We don't live in the same city, so no one notices. Only when we travel to visit them does anyone notice we look alike. I changed my hair and I dress differently so we try to hide how much we are the same.

My family does not think it is too strange about me being a copy, or clone. Yes, it is strange, but they accept it. But I do not think most Dutch people would accept it. Do people accept you in the U.S.?

I look ahead to the next email message and to the post you plan to send to me.

Your friend also, Eline

Brandy read the postal address for Eline at the bottom of the message. It was very confusing to her, nothing like mailing addresses in the U.S..

She forwarded Eline's email message to Sue and then replied to Eline.

Hi Eline,

I'm sending you a quick message to say thank you for sending your postal code. I will email you when we send you a letter so you will know.

Your friend, Brandy

Sue's phone vibrated. She tapped and swiped at it trying to find out why it vibrated. She realized she had a new email message.

She opened the message from Brandy and saw the mailing address for the clone girl from the Netherlands. Sue replied to Brandy, thanking her and telling her that she and the kids would write the letter and would let her know when they were going to drop it in the mail.

She carried the tray of hot chocolate from the kitchen and placed it on the table, warning the kids that the mugs were hot.

She sat down and said to David, "We never had Thanksgiving dinner last year. We had just relocated and life was so complicated a year ago. Besides, I was stuck in that trailer with no room to cook. So, this year we should have a big dinner to celebrate."

"That sounds great," David replied. "But you do not have to cook. You cook every day. Why don't you let me cook the meal?"

"Won't you be watching football? The Chiefs will be on, won't they?"

"I'm not sure," David said. "Yes, there are three football games on Thanksgiving, but I don't know if one of them will include the Chiefs. Usually Dallas and Detroit play, not the Chiefs."

"But you like football, so I'll make the meal," Sue told him.

"You don't have to. I'll be glad to help you. In fact, we can ask Susan and Petunia to pitch in. We can all cook so one person isn't stuck in the kitchen all day."

"Okay, that sounds good. Now, what should we have?"

"Hot Dogs!" Tyler called out.

"You don't eat hot dogs on Thanksgiving, you dummy," Violet replied. "We learned about it in school. You have to eat turkey and corn and yams and pie, just like the pilgrims did."

"Yeah," Kati added, supporting her sister. "No hot dogs."

"There is no fixed meal," David told the kids.

"Ha!" Tyler replied, sticking his tongue out at the girls.

"But we're not eating hot dogs," David told Tyler.

The girls stuck out their tongues at Tyler.

"The first Thanksgiving meal, if there really was such a thing," David said, "was not the same meal as it traditionally is today. Back then, there were probably a lot of root vegetables since they were available in the fall, when the pilgrims celebrated the harvest. They probably didn't eat a lot of turkey and pie."

"They probably didn't watch football, either," Zachary said with a smile.

David laughed at his son. "No, no football."

"So besides hot dogs, which we will not have, what do you kids want? Turkey? Potatoes? Yams?" Sue asked

"Yams?" Kati said. "Ew. I think Mrs. Clark made those once. They were gross."

"She made sweet potatoes, not yams. But since you turned up your nose, we won't make either yams or sweet potatoes. How about corn and stuffing?"

"What's stuffing? Is that like the guts of the turkey?" Tyler asked. "I don't want guts."

"Stuffing is like pieces of bread, dummy," Zachary replied. "You take that and stuff the turkey.

That's why it's called stuffing." To Sue, he said, "Stuffing and corn will be good."

"On the cob?" Kati asked. "I like corn on the cob."

"It's too late for it on the cob, Kati. You can only get it in the summer, fresh from the farmer's field," Violet told her.

"Well, you can get it frozen," David said, "but on the cob is not very good frozen, not like fresh corn in the summer. Corn *off* the cob is good, though."

"Okay, I think we know what we want," Sue said. "I'll talk to Susan and Petunia, and then we'll have lots to eat."

"Do you have to work on Wednesday or Friday?" David asked Sue. "Do you have at least one of those days off? The kids are out of school on Wednesday, Thursday, and Friday."

The kids all cheered.

"I'll ask," Sue told David. "I hope I can have one day off."

Brandy read the reply message from Sue. She nodded to herself.

She sat on the small balcony, soaking up the sun for warmth as she read her book. She smiled at the thought of communicating with Eline.

She's a clone. Another clone. And she's from a different country, The Netherlands! How cool is that? She's smart and plays soccer, like me! I hope I get to meet her in person.

Chapter 10 - It's Just For Fun

Sue woke up on Thanksgiving morning. She smiled. Her arms were wrapped around David.

She could hear the kids downstairs, but did not move a muscle to check on them. She wanted nothing more than to stay in bed.

David also woke to the sounds of the kids, but he, too, did not move.

The two just stared at each other as they embraced.

Eventually, Sue broke the silence by asking David, "I know I surprised you when we were in California, when I talked about marriage. And I didn't mean to surprise you, but it just kind of came out. I just thought it was a good idea."

David smiled.

"So, what do you think?" she asked.

"About?"

"About marriage. What do you think about you and I getting married?"

"Are you sure you want to?" David asked.

"Yes."

"I know you think it's a fun idea, but have you really thought about it? Are you really sure you want to get married?"

"I have thought about it, a lot," Sue replied. "I've thought about it since we went to California. I actually thought about it before going to California, when I thought about Denise having a baby. And yes, I am really sure I want to get married."

"Okay, why?"

"Because I love you. I don't know what that is supposed to feel like, but whenever I'm with you, I'm happy. I want to hug you all the time. I want to hold your hand. I feel like something is missing when I'm not with you. When I'm working, it's okay since I'm so busy, and there are lots of people to talk to. But when I'm not at work, I want to be with you. I want to share everything with you. I want to be a mother with you, with the kids. And I want another child, a baby, too."

David chuckled. "Okay, let's just stick to marriage right now."

"Does this mean you want to?"

"Sue, I'm sixteen years older than you. I've been a bachelor all my life. I've always done my own thing. I've never had any roots to tie me down."

Sue's eyes grew wide and her smile of anticipation turned to a frown. "Does this mean you don't want to?"

"I'd love to," David replied. "Nothing would make me happier."

Sue squealed and squeezed David tighter.

"We're practically married right now," David said. "And with the boys, I have to plant my roots. So I might as well plant them with you, too." He squeezed

Sue a little more tightly, if that was possible.

The noise from the kids on the floor below finally grew to the point that could no longer be ignored. David and Sue knew that if they didn't go down to feed them, they'd soon come up demanding food. David told her, "Remind me to teach Zachary how to make toast and pour orange juice."

After a few kisses, the two unwound their arms and legs, and got out of bed. "You shower," David said, "I'll get the kids."

"I'll be right down," Sue replied.

David walked down the stairs and was quickly swarmed by four, check that, five children. Karen had spent the night, as usual. He made a small amount of breakfast, just enough to hold the kids over until the big meal.

After the kids were fed and returned to the family room, David prepped the turkey that he had thawed and brined the day before. Sue peeled potatoes and prepared the stuffing.

Susan and Petunia joined the group around noon. Having finished his assignment, David switched to the first football game. Zachary hopped on the couch and sat next to his dad while the other, younger kids went upstairs.

When dinner was ready, David sent Zachary to quietly retrieve the kids while he expanded the dining room table to fit all the people as well as the food.

There was no complaining and no fighting during dinner. Everyone talked and laughed, but mostly ate.

After dinner, Petunia and Susan cleaned up, giving David and Sue a break from the kitchen. Sue protested, but David gently guided her out.

Since David was tracking the play in the second football game, the kids couldn't watch TV, and it was too cold to go outside to play, so Sue thought of what to do to entertain the kids. She remembered the letter she had to send to Eline and she needed the kids to be near to write it. "Hey kids," she called out, "let's sit here at the table and do something. I want to practice writing."

A chorus of "Aw, Mom," rang out.

"We'll practice our special language. Remember when we used it last year? We can practice writing it."

"Do we have to?" Zachary asked?

"Yeah, do we have to?" Tyler echoed.

"It will be fun. We can teach Karen how to write it. C'mon."

The kids knew that Sue would not back down when she got an idea, so they reluctantly joined her at the table.

David watched the scene with suspicion. He knew Sue was up to something. But he didn't know what it was.

"Okay," Sue began as she handed out paper and pencils to the kids. "Do you remember what we wrote last year?"

"The Quick Brown Fox," Violet replied.

"Yes," Sue said, adding, "jumped over the lazy dog. Let's practice that." She started writing, hoping the kids would follow her lead.

After a few moments, the kids started showing Sue their work, like she was a teacher at school. "Good," she said. "Nice."

"Show me," Karen said. "I want to see it. Can you teach me?"

The four clone kids showed their papers to

Karen, and explained what each symbol meant. While they were distracted with teaching Karen, Sue wrote more of her letter to Eline. She kept it simple, only saying a few things. There was no point in writing much more she thought. *If the girl can't read our language, there's no point in writing more than this. And if she can, we'll have lots of time to send more letters. This is just a test.*

"What does 'Email Brandy Jackson' mean?" Kati asked, surprising Sue. "Why did you write that, Mommy?"

"Yeah, why did you write that?" Violet asked.

David looked at her with a raised eyebrow.

Sue chuckled nervously. "It's just practicing, she said. I'm just pretending I'm writing an email in our language. It's just for fun."

The girls accepted her explanation, sitting back down to teach Karen more symbols. But David did not. "Just for fun, huh?" David quietly asked Sue.

"Yeah," Sue replied nervously, looking up at David.

"Why do you need to send a letter in your language? You can simply email each other. Why write a paper letter? Are you sending letters to people in the government again? And why do they need to email Brandy?"

"It's nothing," Sue replied.

"Nothing?"

"Yeah, it's just for fun."

"Sue," David whispered, sitting next to her and leaning in close, "If we're going to get married, we have to trust each other."

"I know," she replied with a sigh, her head down. "But I can't tell you right now."

"We can't keep secrets from each other," he

whispered.

"I know," Sue admitted, "but you'll tell Ted. You can't tell Ted… not yet."

"What is it?"

"Do you promise you won't tell Ted?"

David hesitated.

"If we're going to get married…" Sue echoed.

David thought for a moment, and then replied "I promise."

"When Brandy posted the video of Suzanne talking… remember? That was the one that Ted told her to delete. And she did. But someone saw it, a girl in the Netherlands. Her name is Eline. She knows we're clones. She's a clone, too. She knows of nine others in Europe. We're not alone, David. There are more of us clones on the Earth."

David sat for a few seconds before responding, "What's the letter for?"

"We're seeing if Eline can read our language. She's been emailing with Brandy, so Brandy and I want to see if she can read our language also. We want to see if she's just like us."

"You know that you have to be careful."

"I know," Sue replied.

"If Ted's people in the government find out there are other clones around the world, they won't like it. They're nervous enough about you eleven clones. If they find out there are ten more, they'll think it's an invasion or something crazy like that."

"I know."

"Ted has got to know about this."

"Not yet, David. Please, not yet. Just let Brandy and I send this letter. Let us make contact with her before we send the government after her."

"Ted won't send the government after her."

"Are you sure?"

"She's not an American. We can't do anything in her country."

"No, but Ted can have our government contact her government. And then everything will be ruined. What if the Netherland police came here and tried to take us away?"

"I don't think that would happen," David reassured her, "but I see your point." He smiled at Sue. "I'll keep it quiet for now."

Sue smiled and hugged him.

Chapter 11 - Somehow She Knew

Suzanne lay back in her baby seat, babbling contently. Denise and Donald smiled at her, glowing with pride. Their faces brightly reflected the lights from the Christmas tree in their living room.

"That kid is amazing," Juliana announced. "I'm no expert in kids and brain development, although I do have a degree in psychology, but I can tell you that Suzanne is amazing. I mean, she's supposed to be a slug, right? Just drooling and sleeping and eating and pooping, right? But she's way more interactive. Look at her play with that spider toy thing. Sure, she's chewing on it, but she's also pulling at the arms and looking in the mirror. And she's practically talking! I can't get over it."

"She's our special girl," Donald replied.

"Yeah, special," Juliana replied, rolling her eyes.

"Don't forget Brandy," Denise said. "She wasn't a baby, but she learned and developed just as fast. All of the clones did." Turning to Donald, she continued, "Don't you remember when you first were relocated to the base? You all hardly knew anything. And Brandy wanted to hide for the first few days. You all had your own experiences before being moved to the base, but once there, you all learned and grew very quickly."

"That's true," Juliana said. "You clones were all a bunch of misfits, but quickly learned things, how to live, how to take care of yourselves--"

"How to escape," Donald added.

"That's true, Sue did learn how to escape the base, but you all developed so quickly and became great friends."

"You should be proud of yourselves," Denise said, looking first to Donald and then over to Brandy.

Donald smiled.

Brandy wasn't paying attention. She was tapping her phone. "Huh?" she eventually said, noticing the silence. She looked up at the adults. "What?"

Juliana and I were just commenting on how fast all of you clones learned and developed when you first arrived at the base. It's not just Suzanne who learns fast.

"Oh. Okay." Brandy went back to playing with her phone. As she was swiping through her friends pictures, her phoned pinged. "She replied!"

"What's that dear? Who replied?" Denise asked.

"Uh... no one. It's just a friend from school. I thought she was away, but I guess not. It's nothing." Brandy tuned her mother out and started reading the email from Eline.

Hello Brandy,

Happy Christmas! I think that's how you say it in English. Do you celebrate Christmas? We do. But maybe you celebrate Hanukah.

I do apologize for delaying this reply to you. I wanted to wait to get the letter that your friend Sue posted to me. I also was busy with school.

I do say that the letter was interesting. At first, I only saw the symbols. I was unsure what they meant. But then I looked at the letter additional times and I suddenly understood. The quick brown fox jumps over the lazy dog.

"Yes! She can read it!" Brandy called out. She instinctively slapped her hand over her mouth and darted her eyes over to her mother.

"Read what?" Denise asked. "Who can read what?"

Brandy looked at the floor, her eyes moving from side to side, thinking about a response. She dropped her shoulders and sighed. "It's a girl I met online."

"Oh, that's nice," Denise replied.

"She's a clone," Brandy added.

"Oh."

"A clone?" Juliana asked. "As in one of you?"

"Yeah."

"Where? I thought Ted found all of the clones? Did he miss one?" Juliana said.

"The Netherlands," Brandy said. "Eline lives in the Netherlands."

"There's more around the world?" Denise asked, her eyes wide. "You know of more people around the world? How long have you known?"

"Since the visit from the others last month."

"Do you mean to tell me that you've known for almost two months that there are other clones around the world and you never told me?" Denise's face flushed. She scowled at her duaghter, silently accusing her.

"I didn't know what to do! I told Sue, but that's all. I didn't know what to do about it." Tears welled up in Brandy's eyes.

Juliana held up her hand to silence Denise. "Just hang on here. This is not a big deal. Let's stay calm and talk this through."

Denise sat back and took a breath.

"Okay, Brandy, when did you first get a message from this girl?" Juliana asked.

"When the others were here. I posted the video of Su-Su and then deleted it right away after Ted told me to. I swear I did."

Juliana patted her hands toward the ground. "You're not in trouble, Brandy. It's okay. We just want to know what happened."

Brandy wiped the tears from her eyes.

"What did the message say?" Juliana asked.

"She said she knew of a baby that talked early. She asked us if Su-Su was from the goo. She knew. Somehow she knew that Suzanne was a clone." Brandy looked up to Juliana and Denise.

"What else did she say?" Juliana continued.

"She told me that she was from the goo, too. There are like ten people in Europe. And two of the clones in the Netherlands had a baby. That baby talked early too. So I guess that's how she knew."

"So you told her that you're a clone and there are others here?"

"Yeah, was that bad?" Brandy asked, her eyes wide with fear.

"No, that's not bad," Juliana replied. "We just want to know what you told her."

"That's it. I just told her what I like to do."

"But what did you mean when you said she could 'read it'?"

"Sue sent her a letter, written in our language, the clone language. Eline could read it. She can read the same language as we can."

"So Sue knows about all of this?" Denise asked.

"Yeah, just Sue. No one else, I swear."

"It's okay, sweetie," Denise said with a smile. "You're not in any trouble. We just need to know what you told this other person. Everything is good, honey. Everything is good."

Brandy nervously smiled back.

The phone rang. "I'll get it," Donald announced. He stood up and walked to the phone. "Hello? ... Sue! How are you? ... Merry Christmas to you too. How's David? How are the kids? ... That's great. Well, the snow part isn't great, at least not for me, but the rest sounds great. ... Suzanne is excellent."

On cue, Suzanne happily babbled, "Su-Su," from her seat. The ladies laughed.

"She's babbling right now," Donald told Sue, smiling. "We were just talking about how advanced she is and how advanced all of us were when we were first brought together at the base. ... That's true, we were."

"Can I talk to Sue?" Brandy asked her mother. "I need to tell her about Eline. You can listen to what I say, okay?"

"It's fine, Brandy. You're not in trouble. You can even talk to her in your room if you want."

Brandy stood up and walked to the kitchen.

"Hey Sue," Donald told her, "Brandy would like to talk to you. Here she is. ... You too. And I'm sure we'll talk again before then. ... Okay, bye Sue." Donald handed the phone to Brandy.

"Hi Sue. ... Good. I'm good. Listen, I got an email from Eline. ... Yeah, mom knows. She and Juliana both know. I just told them. ... He does? What did he say?"

Denise asked, "Who? Who are you talking about?"

Brandy swatted the air, telling her mother to be quiet. "Yeah, that's the way Mom reacted too. But anyways, I wanted to tell you that she could read it. Eline can read our language! ... Yeah, she got your letter. At first she couldn't read it, but then she kept looking at it and then she got it. She replied by email with the quick brown fox sentence. So she knows what it said. ... I don't know. I haven't read the rest of the message. I'll do that later and I'll let you know."

"Can I talk to Sue?" Denise asked Brandy.

"Mom wants to talk to you, okay Sue? ... Okay, I'll send you an email when I finish reading Eline's message. Okay, bye Sue. ... You too. Here's Mom." Brandy handed the phone to Denise.

"Hello Sue. ... Merry Christmas to you, too. How are the kids? ... Excellent. ... No, you're not in trouble. ... Did I hear that David knows also? ... Can I talk to him for a minute? ... Thanks." Denise waited patiently for David to reply on the other end. "Hi David. ... Same to you. I hear the kids are all doing well. ... She's wonderful. ... Yep, she's still babbling. ... No, she's not talking yet. But who knows? Maybe she will soon. ... David, I just found out about the girl in the Netherlands that Brandy and Sue have been communicating with. Did you know about it? ... Have you told Ted yet? ... Okay, that's good. But we should think about how to tell him. I think this is something he ought to know. ... I don't know. I think it's okay. What's done is done. There's no need to stop the communication."

"Keep talking to this girl, Eline," Juliana called from the couch. "We should find out all we can, just as friends, not as a government official. She'll keep talking to Brandy and Sue."

"Juliana thinks we should let them communicate," Denise told David over the phone. "She thinks that the girl will talk to Brandy and Sue, but might not talk to Ted. ... Okay, sounds good. What are your plans for the holidays?"

While her mother talked, Brandy finished reading the email from Eline.

I'm not sure I know what that means when you talk about the fox. But that is what I read. Did I read it correctly?

I also read the words that Sue wrote. There are four children clones living with her? And who is the David person that she wrote about? Is he a clone also? It sounds like she is very happy.

I hope your holidays are happy, however you celebrate. I look forward to your next email message or written letter.

Your friend, Eline

Brandy tapped a response to Eline.

Hello Eline,

Thank you so much for replying. I'm glad you could read the letter from Sue.

The sentence about the fox has every letter of the alphabet, the English alphabet. Because you were able to read every letter in the sentence, we know that you can read our clone language.

I don't know if you can write the language. We realized that we needed 4 or 5 clones together to be able to write the language. One clone couldn't write the language by themselves. Maybe you could try to write the language.

David is the man who lives in Kansas with Sue. He is not a clone. He knew about us and agreed to be the father for Zach and Tyler. Sue is the mother for Violet and Kati.

We celebrate Christmas here. But I don't really know what it's about. I think there are religious reasons, same as Hanukah, but I don't understand that.

I hope you have happy holidays too! I will keep writing to you by email.

Your friend, Brandy

Chapter 12 - For Now

"Happy new year, Jim!"

"Ted, what a surprise. Happy new year to you. What can I do for you?"

"I'm here in Kansas. I'm almost to your lab. I'm fishing for some results. Do you have any yet?"

"Well, we have portions of the genomes sequenced, but…"

"You're not finished yet."

"Correct."

"Well, can you give me the preliminary results? Can I get a hint?"

"Um, well… we don't really have a presentation ready for you, so…"

"Jim, I don't need a dog-and-pony show. I just want to hear about the results. You can at least tell me, can't you?"

"Yeah, I can do that."

"Okay, good. I'll be outside your building in five to ten minutes. I don't want to see any paper. I just want to talk to you. If you have to bring in the three amigos, please do. And please, nothing formal, Jim."

"Okay, Ted. We'll see you in a few minutes."

"Excellent." Ted ended the call and turned up the radio. He sang along with the tune.

Seven minutes later he pulled into the parking lot of MLS. He got out of the car and put his coat on, but he left his black portfolio in the car. He walked to the front door and was met by Jim. "Good morning."

"C'mon in, Ted. The 'three amigos', as you call them, are waiting in the conference room."

Ted followed Jim into the room and greeted the group leaders. They all sat down around the table.

"Sorry for the last minute visit, but… well, it's kind of what I do, I guess. Anyways, I'd like to know what's happening with the sequencing."

"Bottom line," Jim said, "they're different. Now, we're still analyzing just the first two samples, but they're not the same. One matches an average human genome, the other has differences."

"Explain," Ted said.

"The differences are small and pretty hard to find," Jim said. "It's not like there are huge sequences where they differ."

"It's like there are only a few substitutions here and there," Sarah added.

"Please explain what that means," Ted told her.

"Well, DNA encodes for amino acids to make proteins, right?" Sarah said.

"Yeah."

"Well, there are substitutions for only some of the amino acids. So the proteins are similar, but they're not the same."

"Would this explain the advantages that they

have, or the advantages that you detected in the mice?"

"It might," Cindy replied. "But we can't say for sure. We haven't sequenced the entire genome yet. The substitutions are the differences we've detected so far."

"So, is this why the DNA fingerprints for the clones matched those of their donors last year? Is it because the substitutions don't occur frequently to change the large DNA fragment in the fingerprint?"

"Yes," Bruno said. "The fingerprint looks at huge pieces of DNA. The sequencing is going down to the fine detail. The fingerprint can't detect these little changes."

"The fingerprints showed the clones are the same as their donors. They're human as far as we can see. But we can see small differences in the detailed sequences, and these differences are minor."

"Yeah, that's right," Bruno replied. "Maybe we'll find long sequences with major differences between the two as we continue sequencing. We still have a lot of the genome to sequence."

"Okay, thanks," Ted said. "This is good." He paused, scratching his chin, looking at the table, and then asked, "How hard would it be to screen people for being clones?"

"I'm not sure I follow," Jim said. He frowned in confusion. "Do you mean using the sequencing as a screening test for detecting people who are clones?"

"Yeah. How effective would it be?" Ted asked.

"I'm not sure," Jim said. "If the only differences between native humans and the clones are these minor substitutions, the test would be extremely difficult and very expensive to run. There's no way you could use it to quickly screen for clones."

"Good," Ted said, nodding.

"But," Jim continued, "if we find large sequences that are different between the clones and people, a fluorescent tag could be created that would bind specifically to the clone sequence. That could be a quick diagnostic."

Ted raised one eyebrow. "Hmm."

"Time will tell, Ted. We'll keep sequencing."

"How long will it take you to finish?"

"The computer has kicked out a bunch of sequences that take time to analyze. If we keep it resourced as is, with the same number of people, we should finish with the other three samples in a couple months, April at the latest."

"How's security?"

"We're good. The analysts don't know what they're analyzing."

"Okay, good. Keep up the good work. And remember, none of this gets out," Ted said, looking to each of the four scientists.

"Understood," Jim said. The others nodded.

"Okay, then I'll wait to hear your final report." Ted stood up and smiled. He shook Jim's hand and was escorted out of the building.

After walking to his car, Ted shed his coat and hopped in. He turned up the radio and drove to Enterprise, singing the whole way.

When he pulled into David's driveway, he gave a quick honk of his horn. A few moments later, David opened his front door and looked at the car. Ted got out and waved. He walked through the snow to the front door.

"Ted! What are you doing here?" David asked.

"I just stopped in to say hello."

"C'mon in and sit," David told him. "Can I get you anything? Coffee?"

"Sure, if you got a pot on."

"Coming right up." David went into the kitchen to pour a mug. "Cream? Sugar?"

"Come now, David, after all these months you don't know how I take my coffee? Martha does."

"Sorry, Ted, I usually leave the coffee to the others when we're all together."

"Black. No nothing, just coffee."

David brought Ted his cup and sat down.

"How's the addition to the house coming?" Ted asked. "Are you ready to move in yet?"

"Not yet. The foundation was poured in the fall, before the first frost, and the framing was done. The walls are up, so the weather isn't halting progress. The rest of the job is inside work. We're close, but still have a few weeks to go."

"Is it disrupting Sue's life?"

"Not really. They work weekdays when Sue is at the café and the kids are at school. They have the open walls sealed off, so the mess is minimal. We're used to it, but it will sure be better when it's done."

"I bet," Ted said.

"So, you're just here to say hello?" David asked.

"I was in Manhattan, to visit the lab."

"And?"

"Testing is progressing."

"Any results?"

"The lab has found differences," Ted replied. "They can't say exactly what those differences are, you know, what they mean. But the clone DNA is different."

"Huh," David replied as he sat and thought

about the news.

Ted calmly took another sip of his coffee. "Do you have any news for me?"

"Uh…" David said, "not really." He shrugged his shoulders. "Things are back to normal after the holidays."

"You hesitated," Ted said. "You say nothing, but there is something."

"Nah."

"David, I know there's something to tell me."

"I, uh, can't tell you."

Ted's eyes popped. "And why not?"

"I promised Sue," David replied.

Ted shook his head in disbelief and stared at David, his palms turned up.

"I promised Sue I wouldn't tell you."

Ted's eyebrows raised and he tilted his forehead forward. "You promised?"

"We're engaged, or we soon will be, officially," David said. "We have to be able to trust each other. I told her she couldn't keep secrets from me and, in turn, she told me I couldn't tell you."

"And you're staying true to your word," Ted confirmed.

"Yes."

"Because you're engaged."

"Yes."

"Should I be concerned?" Ted asked.

"About the engagement?"

"No, about whatever it is that you're not telling me. Should I be concerned about that?"

"I don't know," David replied.

"Use your best judgment."

"I don't think so. Not right now."

"When?"

"I don't know."

"When will you know?"

"Ted, please trust me. I think you know enough about me and my past to know that I'll tell you when I need to. I don't think it's time. Nothing has happened. And I don't think anything will. For now, I can't tell you. Sue would be so mad, and I don't want that. But if it gets to a point when you need to know, I'll tell you."

Ted glared at David, testing his resolve. "Okay, I trust you," he concluded. "For now."

Chapter 13 - Aki

Hello Brandy,

I'm sorry I haven't written to you for a time. The holidays were full of activity for me and my family.

Happy new year to you. I wish that your holidays were merry.

I want to tell you that I have included messages from other clones that I have communicated with. They are sending greetings to you. We all speak English as another language, so they sent messages in English. (of course, the people in England speak English. lol) I'm hoping you enjoy them.

As you will view below, I have made contact with a clone from Japan. He is a young man. He is a computer person who found me on the internet. He is not accepted in his country so he is hiding I think. But he knows about us and I told him about you and the others in the United States.

As I keep looking I find more clones around the world. I am hoping that you are finding this fun as I do.

Your friend, Eline.

Brandy's eyes scanned the brief messages from the other clones. "Wow," she whispered. "Eline made contact with all these people. They found each other and now they're finding us."

She used her fingers to count the number of people that Eline told her about. "With the guy in Japan, that's twelve other clones. So with the eleven of us... well, twelve with Suzanne, there are twenty four clones that we know of. Who would have thought there would be that many of us?"

She sat back against her bed, thinking about her arrival, and the day she met the others at the base. *And now I have email messages from others around the world!* "I have to tell Sue," she said aloud. She typed an email message.

Hi Sue,

I got an email from Eline. She included messages from other clones around the world, even one from a guy in Japan.

They all seem like nice people. Their messages were polite and friendly. They are all interested in meeting all of us.

I'll forward Eline's message to you so you can read it.

This is exciting. There are twenty four of us clones on Earth! And there may be more!

Talk to you soon!

She tapped the send button and forwarded the email from Eline. She was about to set her phone down when it pinged with a new email message.

Brandy saw the sender's name: Aki Nakami. When she opened the message, all she saw were characters. "Great, I just got spammed by some dude in China." She was about to delete the message when she looked again at the characters. "Wait! I can read this!" she said aloud. "But I can't read Chinese."

She focused carefully on the symbols and the words instantly popped off the screen.

Ms. Brandy Jackson

I am writing to introduce me to you. My name is Aki. It means autumn. My surname is Nakami. It means substance. I was gave this name by Japan government because I was clone from substance that was in Japan in the autumn of the year one year before.

I am one of three people from the substance. Japan government gave us job and home. Other Japan people do not know of us.

I attached a font program to this email letter. Download the program. It will translate English to clone language. Select clone font in email program and type letter in English. The program translates to clone language. I used the scanned letter from Ms. Eline van der Bach to make the program. I used the quick brown fox jumped over the lazy dog to know the characters that translates to English characters. I have also sent the program to Ms. Eline.

I do wish you send me a reply letter.

Aki Nakami

Brandy set her phone down on the floor, got up to get her laptop, and turned it on. She waited for it to boot up, and then opened the email from Aki. She downloaded the program and installed it.

This is exciting! I have to see if it works! I'll send a letter to Sue.

She composed a short message to Sue. As instructed, she selected "clone" as the font to use, and began to type her message. On her screen, the clone characters corresponding to letters appeared on the screen. She explained to Sue about Aki and the program he sent, and how she had used it to write the email in the clone language. She clicked the send button, and then forwarded Aki's message containing the program.

Chapter 14 - It's Time

After cleaning up the dishes from lunch, David sat on the couch in the living room to watch the football game. The Chiefs didn't make the playoffs, but he was happy to watch other teams.

The kids were upstairs playing quietly, so Sue took the opportunity to check her email. She brought her laptop into the living room and sat next to David. When her email opened, she saw the new email in her inbox. "Four messages," she said aloud.

"From who?" David asked.

"All from Brandy," Sue replied. She quietly started reading the first. "Wow." Her eyes popped. "Twenty four," she said.

"Twenty four what?"

"Twenty four clones that we know about. Brandy's friend, Eline, has found twelve other clones. Those twelve plus the twelve of us are twenty four. And they wrote messages to Brandy to say hello."

Sue opened the second message and read the forwarded messages from the other clones around the world. "These are nice."

"What are?"

"The messages from the other people."

"Do you mean that they all wrote to Brandy to say hello?"

"Yeah. Well, not all of them, but a lot of them. They all wrote to Brandy through the girl in the Netherlands. She sent the emails to Brandy in one message."

"So it's not just Brandy and this Eline girl talking to each other? It's the twelve others talking to Brandy?"

"Yeah. It's exciting!" She took hold of David's arm and lightly shook it. "Isn't this exciting?"

"I'm not so sure," David replied.

"Why not?" Sue asked, frowning "Why don't you think it's exciting?"

"A lot of communication back and forth might make people nervous."

"You mean Ted?"

"Well, I was actually thinking about the committee that he reports to, but yes, Ted would probably be nervous too, because of the committee."

"But they know about us. They know about our letters last year, to the Secretary of the Interior. And the First Lady even knows about us. Most people don't know we're clones, but they do. They haven't done anything about it, so why would they be nervous?"

"They think you clones here in the U.S. are the only clones on the planet. And they think you're controlled. But if twelve other clones are introduced, that might make them nervous about controlling all of you."

"They won't do anything," Sue said confidently.

She opened the third message and immediately called out, "Whoa."

"What?"

"Look." She turned her computer so David could see the text on the screen.

"What is that? Is that Chinese?"

"It's our language, the clone language. Brandy sent me a message written in our language."

"How can that be? I thought there have to be four or five clones together to write. There are only three clones in Burbank, and one of them is a baby."

"I don't know. Let me read her message." Sue's eyes followed the characters on the screen. "There is a program that a clone man in Japan created that translates English to our language," she told David. "He used the letter I sent to Eline, the paper copy, to know how to translate letters to characters. Brandy forwarded his email with the program attached. This is cool! Now we can all type in our language. We don't need four or five of us together. We can send messages in our language! Isn't that cool?"

David muted the TV. "Let me get this straight," he began, "a man in Japan, a clone, took the letter that you sent to the girl in the Netherlands and was able to use the characters to create a computer program that will translate English into your clone language? And you can type in English and it will show your language?"

"I guess. Let me see." Sue focused on her computer, reading the instructions from Aki, and downloaded the program. She opened a new message, selected the clone font, and began typing. She jumped in her seat and shrieked. "It works!"

David leaned into Sue and watched as she typed. Her fingers struck the letter keys, but the strange squiggly characters appeared on the screen. "Huh."

"I gotta tell the others," Sue announced. She deleted the text and started a new message. She typed fast, quickly addressing the email to the other clones, and sent the message. "I have to forward the program," she added. She typed and clicked a bit more and then was finished. "This is so exciting!"

"Sue," David said, "it's time to tell Ted."

She jerked her head toward him and stared.

"He needs to know what is happening. If it was just you eleven clones here in the U.S., it wouldn't be a concern. And maybe just the girl in the Netherlands would be okay, but it's gone beyond that."

"Ted does not need to know. We're just saying hello to each other. That's it."

"Right now you're just saying hello. But you also have a coded language. And you're not going to stop at 'hello'. You're going to continue to share information."

"So?"

"Remember when the FBI saw the letters you wrote to the Secretary of the Interior?"

"Yeah."

"They didn't like it. And the more you find out about the other clones, the more you share information, the more dangerous you might appear to those who are watching."

"Watching? Who's watching? Who would care about some emails between friends?"

"I can think of a lot of people. And those people will not want you all sharing information with others around the world, especially in a coded language."

"Don't be silly, David. What harm can we do?"

"Sue, I have to tell Ted."

"Don't," she replied, a scowl on her face. "You promised me, David. You promised you wouldn't tell Ted. You said we had to trust each other."

"I did," David calmly replied. "But Ted has to know about this. He can't be caught off guard. He may not do anything about it, but he must know what's happening."

"David, no."

"I have to, Sue."

Sue continued to scowl.

David's cell phone rang. "Hello? ... Denise? ... Yes, I'm sitting with Sue right now, looking at the email from the clone in Japan. ... I had no idea until just now. Well, that's not true. I knew about the girl, but not the translation program. ... I agree, Ted needs to know."

"He does not," Sue called out, loud enough for Denise to hear on the other end of the call.

"Yeah, that's Sue. ... Hang on, here she is." He handed the phone to Sue.

"Ted does not need to know," Sue argued. She listened to Denise, interjecting with "but" and "well", trying to defend her position. "I understand," she finally said. Defeated, she handed the phone back to David.

"Hi Denise," he said flatly. "Yeah, I'll call him. ... I agree. It is for the best. Ted will keep it quiet. ... No, I see no reason why they have to stop. Ted may disagree, but I think it's okay. ... Okay, say hi to Donald and Juliana and Brandy. ... Talk to you soon."

Sue sat on the couch, her arms crossed, pouting,

when David ended the call. She didn't say anything.

"Ted needs to know," David said quietly.

Sue remained quiet, but sighed. She knew David was correct.

David dialed Ted's number. "I'll put it on speaker so you can hear, okay?" he asked Sue.

She nodded.

"Hello?" Ted answered.

"Hi Ted, it's David."

"On a Sunday? What's up?"

"Remember when you stopped by a couple weeks ago and I said it wasn't time to tell you something?"

"Yeah..."

"Well, it's time," David told him.

"Okay... What is it?"

"Brandy and Sue have made contact with other clones, in other countries."

"You're kidding, right?"

"No, Ted, I'm not."

"Okay, tell me more."

"The first contact occurred when we were all in California. The video that Brandy posted--"

"Just for a couple minutes," Sue jumped in. "She deleted it, just as you told her to, Ted."

David patted his hand in the air, telling Sue to be quiet. "Someone, a girl in the Netherlands, saw the video in the short time that is was available. And that girl contacted Brandy. They've been sharing emails. Sue knows about the girl, too. Brandy confided in Sue."

"And..."

"She's a clone. And she knows of at least eleven other clones around the world."

There was no sound on the other end of the phone.

"They've shared emails between each other," David continued. "And get this, one of those clones, someone in Japan, created a computer program to translate English into the clone language. I saw Sue load it and use it. When she typed letters on the keyboard, the clone characters appeared on the screen."

[*silence*]

"Hello? Ted? You still there?"

"I'm here," Ted said calmly. He waited a few moments before responding. "Stop emailing."

"What?" Sue called out. "No way. We need to continue to learn more about these new clones."

"Sue!" Ted replied. "No! Do not send another email. *Call* the others and tell them not to send any more emails to anyone. No more email."

"But--"

"Sue! No. More. Email."

Chapter 15 - Follow the Rules

Denise knocked on the door and then opened it slowly. "Are you ready Brandy?"

"Dee-Dee!" Suzanne added as she sat, perched against Denise's hip.

"Yeah, almost," Brandy replied flatly.

"Do you have the bag, Donald?" Denise asked.

"Yes, dear, I have the bag," Donald replied with a sigh. "We've gone over this at least twice just this morning."

"I know, I know. But this is a big day. It's her first trip to the children's museum." She looked at her daughter and said, in mommy talk, "Isn't that right sweetie? Yes, we're going to the museum."

Suzanne cackled with glee at the sound of her mother's voice.

"Jeez mom, she's four months old. She's still a slug. She can't even crawl on her own yet. It's way too early for her. She won't get anything out of this."

"Maybe not," Denise admitted, "but we don't get a chance to get out of the house a lot, so I thought this would be a good way to get her out. It's not warm enough to go to a park, so this is the next best option."

"Yeah, but it'll be totally boring. Can't I hang with my friends?"

"Don't be such a downer," Denise replied, waving her hand at Brandy.

Suzanne waved her hand, copying her mother.

"Fine, whatever."

Juliana entered the condo through the front door. "Good morning," she called out.

Denise and Donald greeted her and began to get Suzanne and her things ready to go. Brandy slowly walked out of her room, looking bored.

"Yo, Sis," Juliana said to Brandy. "What's up? What's wrong?"

"I gotta go to the museum."

"Yeah, but it'll be fun," Juliana replied.

"Uh, no. Suzanne is way too young. She's just gonna lay there and do nothing. And so I have to suffer."

"Oh, it won't be that bad. It'll be fun. Besides, Su-Su may surprise you."

"Su-Su!" the baby said from her car seat.

"C'mon folks," Donald called out, "time to go." He walked out the door carrying the car seat. The others followed.

Once the baby and all of her stuff were extracted from the car, the proud parents carried her into the museum, with Aunt Julie right behind.

Brandy lagged back, not interested. She checked her accounts. *Nothing... Nothing... Boring... Hey! Another email from Eline!* She read the message.

Dear Brandy,

I have not received an email from you or the others in many weeks. Is something wrong with you? I hope I did not anger you.

Please write back to me if you are able to and if you want to.

Your friend, Eline

She's mad at me. Or she's disappointed, at least. I gotta reply. I know Ted said not to, but you can't just abandon a friend like this. I gotta at least say hello and tell her why I haven't been writing. She started tapping.

Hello Eline,

I know it's been many weeks since I last wrote to you and I'm sorry. I want to write to you, but I'm not really allowed to. The government man who knows about us in the U.S. doesn't want us communicating with you. And not just you, but all the other clones.

I'm sorry.

Brandy

She put her phone away and went to find the others. She looked in tunnels and checked in all the nooks and crannies of the exhibits. She finally found them in a sandbox, all of them.

Suzanne was playing in the sand, filling up containers as they were handed to her by the three doting adults.

Brandy noticed she was sitting upright. "Since when does she sit up? She's only four months old. She should still be a slug."

"I know," Juliana replied. This is unusual. Of

course, nothing is really unusual with Su-Su."

"Su-Su!"

Brandy took out her phone and clicked a picture of her baby sister, sitting in the sandbox, happily filling colored plastic containers with sand. The phone vibrated in her hands, notifying her of a new tweet. She swiped and tapped and found the direct message.

> @bjack1313 Hello Brandy. I'm sad to see that you cannot email me.

Brandy replied:

> @eline913 I don't like it. But I'm trying to follow the rules.

> @bjack1313 You are following the rules. You are not emailing me by Twitter

> @eline 913 You're right! He didn't say no texting or twitter. So yay!

> @bjack1313 How are you? How is your sister, the new baby?

> @eline913 Ugh. Everything is about the baby. Baby this, baby that

> @bjack1313 Do you not like your sister?

> @eline913 No, I do like her. But she gets all the attention.

@bjack1313 What has she done?
Does she continue to talk? Is she
saying more words?

@eline913 Yeah she still talks. She
says our names. And now she's
sitting on her own. I don't think
she's supposed to sit by herself.
She's only 4 months old

@bjack1313 The baby here talked
and sat up early also. She did a lot
of things earlier than other babies

@eline913 It looks like Suzanne is
just like the other clone baby

@bjack1313 We should compare
the two babies to see if they are the
same in all ways. Send me direct
messages telling me what she does

@eline913 Ok. I'm sending you a
picture that I just took of her sitting
up. She looks normal, but she's not.

@bjack1313 I hope you can email
me soon. I have many things to
share.

@eline913 I hope so too. Maybe in
a week or two I can send an email
and we can talk again.

@bjack1313 Good. I would like
that. I hope to talk with you soon.
Goodnight friend.

@eline913 Goodnight friend

When Brandy looked up from her phone, the
others were gone. Brandy wandered around until she
found them, this time playing in water.

"Sis," Juliana called out, "Can you take a picture
of Suzanne? She's so cute."

"Su-Su!"

Brandy laughed at her sister while she took a
few pictures. "She's soaked!"

"Dee-Dee!" Suzanne said, looking at her big
sister and smiling.

Brandy lowered her phone and smiled back.

Chapter 16 - The Rules Have Changed

"I'm going to send an email to that Aki guy in Japan," Sue quietly told herself. "I don't care what Ted says. We're just learning about other people. He didn't care when I read books after I first arrived. And he was the one that gave us all computers at the base. So why does he care?"

She composed a new message.

Hello Mr. Nakami,

It's an honor to meet you.

My name is Sue Cook. I am a mother of two daughters. I live in Enterprise, Kansas, which is located in the middle of the United States.

As you know, I am a clone. I arrived here in the U.S. at the same time as the other clones, including Brandy Jackson. I think that we arrived at the same time as you did in Japan, and as Eline van der Bach and the others did in Europe. We all arrived from the substance. We call it "goo".

Please tell me about yourself. What happened when you arrived? Can you tell me? What do you do now? I understand that you know how to program computers because you were able to create the clone language program. I am very interested to learn about you and the other clones around the world.

Please send a reply. Thank you.

Your new friend, Sue

She reviewed the message, as it appeared in the clone language on the screen. She nodded and clicked the send button.

"There."

While he was typing, a notification popped up on his screen. His eyes widened and he jumped back in his seat. *An email! From America!*

Aki read the email and smiled. He saw the characters that he created and was pleased that someone had used his program to reply. He composed a reply.

Hello Ms. Sue,

I am glad to meet you. It is honor to meet another clone. And you are from America, which is very big honor. Thank you for using the program.

I arrive at the same time as Ms. Eline in the Netherlands, and I believe you arrive at the same time. We all arrive when the goo landed on the Earth.

When I was found, I was taken by the government. I was given government job and live in government apartment. I am free to do activities outside of work.

I like computers. I quickly learn to program. I program well. I also like to research about life outside of Japan. I use the internet. I have learned many things about the United States and Europe. I know many details about the other parts of the world. I am not permitted to travel, but I would like to travel.

Please continue to send email messages to me. I enjoy reading about you and other clones living in America.

Your clone friend, Aki

After he clicked the send button, he found the message in his sent folder and forwarded it to the other two clones in Japan. He also included Eline in the addressee list. He wrote:

To all,

I am forwarding message I received from America. It is from Ms. Sue Cook in Kansas. You will also see my response. I hope we can share the messages from around the world as I started with Ms. Eline.

Your clone friend, Aki

Eline finished surfing, checking Twitter and Instagram. As she turned out the light and set her phone down, it vibrated.

An email from Aki! She sat up in bed and read the message. The light from the screen lit her eyes as they followed the lines of clone characters. She smiled. *The rules in America have changed! I can email Brandy!*

She clicked the forward button and addressed Aki's message to Brandy. She added her own message.

Hello Brandy,

I see that you in America are now able to email other clones. I am pleased. I have been wanting to write to you and tell you all that I have learned recently.

The other clone baby that lives here in the Netherlands, her name is Lotta. Her mother and father told me she was born in September. That was one year after we arrived. She is now five months old. She is one month more old than your sister. She started moving without help. You call it crawling? She surprised her mother and father. Maybe your sister will soon be crawling without help.

The clones in Europe are all writing in the clone language that Aki sent to us. I have been writing to Aki. All of the clones have a similar beginning. We arrived when our people touched the slime. Our governments took us originally. Most governments let us live freely, like the Netherlands. But the government still watches us. But in Japan, Aki and the two other men are watched more than us. I think Aki said this to your friend Sue in his email message. But he is able to send emails freely.

I wish that we could all meet. I know that will

not be possible, but I want to. I hope that you want to meet me.

Please continue to email and tell me about you and your sister. Also please tell the other clones in the United States to email the others and tell us of their stories. The more information we learn is better.

Your happy friend, Eline

Before she clicked the send button, she added the email addresses of the other clones in Europe and Japan.

Brandy was sitting at the kitchen table, eating lunch, when her phone vibrated. She instinctively took it out of her pocket and looked at it. Her eyes popped.

"No phones at the table," Denise reminded her.

Brandy didn't argue. Rather, she continued staring at her phone, ignoring her mother.

"Brandy," her mother scolded.

"Dee-Dee," her sister added for effect.

"Did you hear you mom?" Donald asked.

Brandy didn't respond.

"Hello? Little sis', you in there?" Juliana asked, giving Brandy a little tap with her fork.

"Huh?" She looked around the table.

"Please put your phone away," Denise said.

"But I got an email from Eline," she replied.

"I don't care. You can read it later."

"But she forwarded a message from Aki in Japan. And his message came from *Sue*. We must be able to send emails now, I guess. Eline sent it to, like, everyone in Europe and Japan. She asked me to send it to everyone here in the U.S. so we can all share."

"Ted didn't say we could send email messages," Denise announced. She looked to Donald and Juliana. "Did he?"

Donald shrugged. Juliana shook her head.

"Eline told me about the baby in the Netherlands," Brandy told her mom. "She's a clone baby, like Suzanne--"

"Su-Su!" the baby called out, cackling with delight at the sound of her name.

"The other baby is five months old. She's crawling already. She talked like Su-Su and sat up like her very early. Eline wants to compare the stuff that Lotta, that's her name, does to the stuff that Suzanne does."

"La-La!" Suzanne called out.

Chapter 17 - It's About Time

"Well, that should take care of everything," the contractor said.

Sue's face broke into a huge smile. She hopped in place with excitement.

"The sod in the yard will hopefully take root," he told Sue. "If not, you can always call us and we'll come back and replace it. At least you won't be outside too much in the next few weeks, at least not until April. Just be careful if you walk on it."

"We will," Sue said, the smile still plastered on her face. "And thank you!"

"You're welcome, Sue," he replied. Then he laughed. "I don't get to know many customers as well as we all got to know you, Sue. Of course, not many people are as excited about construction as you."

She blushed.

"I hope you enjoy your new house."

"I will," she said.

"We will," David said, standing just behind Sue. He put his hand on her shoulder.

"We definitely will," Sue added.

The contractor shook their hands and walked to his truck. He turned around on the loop in the driveway and drove toward the street.

With the smile still on her face, and still hopping in place, Sue said, "It's done! It's finally done! You and the boys can move in!"

"I scheduled the movers for tomorrow," David said with a sly grin.

"You did? They're coming tomorrow?" Sue squealed and ran in circles. Then she launched herself at David, hugging him tightly.

"It's kind of cold out here," David said. "Should we go inside?"

Sue kissed him and replied, "Absolutely."

The kids were playing quietly inside when the two entered the kitchen. "Is it done?" Zachary asked. "Can we move in soon?"

"Yep, it's done," David replied. "And the movers come tomorrow."

"Yesss!" Zachary said, pumping his fist.

"Yea!" Tyler said.

Turning to David, Sue asked, "Should we tell them?"

"Tell us what?" Kati replied.

"Yeah, tell us what?" Tyler echoed.

David nodded to Sue.

"Well, now that the house is finished and you men will be moving in tomorrow," Sue began, "it's like we're one big family now. We each have our own rooms, but we're all under one roof."

"Yeah..." Violet said. "So...?"

"Well, you see... David and I are, well, in love with each other and, well... We don't want this to affect anything…"

"What?" Zachary said impatiently.

Sue took a breath and then told the kids, "David and I are getting married."

"Finally," Violet said.

"Yeah, it's about time you told us," Zachary said, rolling his eyes.

"Duh, we all knew, Mom," Kati replied.

Sue looked at David.

"I told you they knew," David replied.

"Did you tell them?"

"Nope, but it's not too difficult to figure out."

"Oh, okay," Sue said. She turned back to the kids. "Now that it's official, we need to set a date."

"Next week," Kati offered.

"Um, that's a little early," David said. "We need to plan a lot of things. And we need to give everyone time to make travel plans. And we can't do it until you kids are out of school, including Brandy."

"You mean everyone's coming? As in *everyone*?" Violet confirmed.

"Everyone," Sue replied.

The kids shouted with happiness.

"When are you going to tell everyone?" Zachary asked.

"We thought we'd call tonight, after dinner," David replied.

"Speaking of dinner…" Sue said.

Karen knocked on the door and proceeded to enter. She was a regular guest in the house and had her own protocol for entry.

"Guess what!" Kati hollered when Karen came into view. "Mom and David are getting married!"

"Yea! It's about time," Karen replied as she

walked over to play with the other kids.

Susan and Petunia entered the kitchen and congratulated Sue and David. "We're so happy for you," Susan told them.

"You two make a perfect couple," Petunia added. "It's like you were made for each other."

"Who would've thought?" Sue said, smiling.

"When's the date?" Susan asked her clone.

"The end of June, one of the last two weekends," Sue replied. "We'll have to make sure everyone can make it. We'll call the others after dinner and see which weekend will work the best."

"Well, let's get cooking then," Petunia said.

The group had a happy dinner together, celebrating the completed house and the pending marriage.

After dinner, the kids went upstairs to play. Along the way they argued about in which room they'd play. The boys suggested their new, non-pink rooms.

"David," Petunia said, "let Susan and I do the dishes tonight. You and Sue have some phone calls to make." David protested, but Petunia took the dish brush from his hand and said, "Consider it an early wedding present." She smiled at him.

He returned the smile and dried his hands.

Sue picked up her phone and started dialing. David sat with her at the table.

"Hello, Denise? ... How are you? How's the family, Brandy, Donald, and that cute little baby? ... Is that her that I hear in the background? Wow, she really is talkative, isn't she? Has she said any actual words yet? ... Don't worry, she will soon."

Sue pulled the phone away from her face and told David, "She really is babbling a lot. That baby is going to talk any day, I can tell." She smiled with pride, the clone genes in effect within her namesake.

"So Denise, we're calling to tell you something. ... Yes, the house is finished, which *is* good news, but we have something else--" Her eyes popped. "How did you know?

David chuckled in his chair. He quietly said, "It's not that hard to figure out."

"So we want to set a date. We're thinking the end of June. When is Brandy out of school? ... Great! So there will be no problem with your schedule. We're thinking the second-to-last weekend, not the one just before the Fourth of July. Will that work for you? ... Okay, check it out and call us back. But we'll plan on that. ... Thank you, thank you. We're so happy. Say hello to everyone there, including Juliana, and give that little baby a squeeze from me. ... Talk to you soon! ... Okay, goodbye Denise!"

"She seemed happy," David said. "Is everything good in California?"

"How did she know?" Sue asked, mainly to herself. "Is it that obvious?"

"It's logical," David told her.

Susan turned to them, smiled, and added with a nod, "It's that obvious."

Sue blushed and smiled.

Chapter 18 - Someday Maybe

Hello Brandy,

It has been some time since we last sent email. How are you? Did you celebrate Saint Patrick's Day? We don't celebrate it here as a national holiday, but some of us still wear green. Some people think it is a good day to drink more alcohol. The other clones in the UK celebrated the holiday more than I did.

I have been talking with the other clones. I have included them as cc: on this message. We all think it would be a good idea if we could all meet. We know that it would be impossible to meet, all of us, but we still think it would be a good idea. What do you in America think?

I wanted to tell you about Lotta, the baby here in the Netherlands. She is pulling herself up and standing now. But only for a little time. She falls a lot. lol Her parents say that it is early to be trying to stand. She is only 6 months old. Has your sister begun to crawl yet? Please tell me. I am curious.

When does your school end? We have to stay in school until July. We resume classes in September. We have many holidays during the year. Is that the same as in the U.S.?

Here in the Netherlands, the spring season is arriving. The temperatures are rising to close to 10 degrees right now. That's in Celsius, of course. The chance of freezing temperatures, below zero, is very low now. But it is still not warm yet. How hot does it get in California in the summer time? I am curious. It can be as high as 25 here, sometimes close to 30.

I hope that you are doing well in school. Please reply and we can continue to share with each other. Remember to include the clones in America.

Your friend, Eline

Brandy took her cell phone into the family room where Denise and Donald were playing with Suzanne on the floor. Juliana had come over to visit, as she usually did. "Hey Mom," Brandy asked, "how do you get Fahrenheit from Celsius?"

"I'm not sure," Denise replied. "I know that zero in Celsius is thirty-two in Fahrenheit, the freezing point of water, but that's about it. Look it up online."

"Ugh," Brandy replied. "That's such a pain. Can't you just tell me?"

"I don't know how to convert one to the other," Denise said.

"You have to multiply by nine and divide by five," Juliana said. "And then you have to add or subtract thirty-two. But I'm not sure which. I seem to recall that body temperature, ninety-eight point six in Fahrenheit, is thirty-seven in Celsius."

"I'll look it up," Brandy said flatly.

"Why do you ask?" Denise said.

"I got an email from Eline. She told me how hot and cold it is in the Netherlands, in Celsius. I want to know what that is in Fahrenheit."

"I don't like you emailing with that Eline girl. Ted told us to stop emailing. Yet Sue went ahead and did it anyway. She shouldn't have done that."

"Mom, it's no big deal. We're just saying hi and comparing the weather and school," Brandy said. "Oh, and she tells me about what Lotta does."

"La-La!" Suzanne called out.

Her parents and Juliana laughed.

"Lotta's pulling herself up and trying to walk," Brandy told them. "She falls a lot. But she's only one month older than Suzanne."

"Su-Su!" the baby echoed.

"And she's crawling now," Brandy said, pointing to her sister. "So maybe in a month *she'll* be pulling herself up."

"Maybe," Denise said. "But I still don't like it that you're emailing that girl."

"Mom, chill. It's no big deal. We're not doing anything except comparing life here and there." She turned and returned to her room. She searched how to convert from Celsius to Fahrenheit. She typed in the temperatures that Eline gave her. "Wow, it's cold there. And it doesn't even get warm there in the summer."

She tapped the *reply all* button on her phone and added the email addresses of Patsy and Sue to the cc: line of the message.

Dear Eline,

I am good. No, we didn't celebrate St. Patrick's Day. I can't drink alcohol and I didn't wear green, so it was a normal day for me.

You have cold weather in the Netherlands. It's much warmer here in California. Right now, the temperatures are around 70 during the day, that's like 20 for you. In the summer, we get up to 100 some times. Mostly 80 or 90. That's like 30 or 40 to you. But other parts of the country are colder than California. In Kansas, where Sue lives, it's 40 or 50 right now. That's about the same as the temperatures you have in the Netherlands. In the summer, Kansas can get just as hot as California. I think since you are close to the ocean, you have cooler temperatures.

Our school year ends in early June. We go back to school at the end of August. I think our school years are close to each other. We get vacation at Christmas and in the spring.

Suzanne, my sister, is crawling, just like you said Lotta was a month ago, so I guess that she will be standing soon. She's a funny baby. She's happy all the time. I like her. But I don't like to change her diapers. Yuk.

I agree about meeting each other. I think it's a good idea. But I don't think it will be possible. I think our governments won't let us travel to other countries. We can dream about it. Someday maybe.

Your friend, Brandy

Chapter 19 - No One Else Knows

Ted pulled into the driveway to David's house. He was about to get out when he hit himself on the forehead. "Duh, they don't live here anymore. C'mon Ted." He shook his head in disgust. He backed the car out of the David's driveway, drove a few yards down the road, and pulled into the long driveway leading to Sue's house.

When he parked, he got out of the car and took the gift from the back seat. He walked up the path and rang the doorbell.

"Ted!" rang out from the house. Sue threw the door open. "Welcome to our house!" She held the door and motioned for him to enter.

"Hello, Sue. You have a lovely house," Ted said with a smile.

"Well yeah, you built it for me!"

"Hi Ted," David said, as his guest walked into the kitchen. "Welcome."

"I have to admit that I first pulled into your driveway," Ted told David. "I had to back out and pull in the right one." He laughed at himself. "We're gonna have to get rid of that other house. It's too confusing."

"Seriously?" Sue asked.

"Actually, yes," Ted replied plainly.

"Is it really that confusing?" she asked.

"Well no, not really," Ted replied with a smile. "But I did promise to remove the other house once we had built this one. You see, we bent the zoning laws a little to allow two houses on this one lot."

"Huh," David replied.

"Now, when do I get the full tour?" Ted asked.

"Right now," Sue replied. "C'mon." She led Ted around the house, showing him all of the rooms, original and recently-added.

When they returned to the kitchen, Ted said, "It looks like you're missing a kid."

David scowled at him in confusion.

"Where's Karen? Isn't she always here?"

David laughed. "Yeah, she's almost always here. I think you should have added one extra room for her."

"Nope. What you got now is all you get. That's it. No more additions," Ted replied, shaking his head.

"Karen will be here soon, with Susan and Petunia," Sue told Ted.

"Okay," Ted replied. "While we have time, I brought you a little house-warming gift." He handed the box to Sue.

"You shouldn't have," David told him.

"Yeah, he should have," Sue shot back. "Just kidding!" she added with a grin.

Sue unwrapped the gift. It was a box of assorted bath salts and scented candles.

"I thought you two, as new homeowners and soon-to-be newlyweds could use a few things to get some quiet alone-time together."

"What are you trying to tell us?" Sue asked.

"You two should enjoy each other together," Ted replied. "I figured your bathtub was the best place for you two to hide."

"How romantic," David said, looking at Ted. "It's a little out of character for you, though, isn't it?"

"Well, I thought of buying you two noise-cancelling headphones to wear around the house, but that's wasn't nearly as cozy," Ted said with his sly grin.

A knock at the door signaled the arrival of the ladies from across the street.

Karen ran upstairs to join the other kids, while Susan and Petunia carried in supplies. David took the food, allowing Susan and Petunia to greet Sue and Ted.

When dinner was ready, Sue called the kids, who thundered down the hall and down the stairs.

"So Sue," Ted began while they ate, "should I be arranging a flight for the second-to-last weekend in June?"

"Are you going to fly everyone here?" she asked, surprised at the offer.

"Yeah," Ted replied. "It's cheaper to use the jet than it is to pay to fly everyone here. Besides, this is a big occasion. We'll spare no expense for the wedding of Sue."

Sue beamed with happiness. She clapped her hands and bounced in her seat. "I'm so excited!"

"I don't know if she'll make it as long as June. That's almost three months from now," David said to Ted.

"I know!" Sue replied.

While cleaning up after the meal, Susan asked Ted, "What brings you out here?"

"I'm glad you asked," he replied. "I'm going to the lab tomorrow. They have the DNA results."

Susan sat up in her chair. "Oh my god, I almost forgot about that. Will you tell us the results?"

"Yes, I'll let you know. I won't put anything in writing, but I'll get the results to you somehow."

"I want to know what the tests showed," Sue said. "I hope it says we're totally normal, no differences. I liked knowing that we were human, just like our donors. That's why you let us go, Ted."

Ted nodded.

"I hope it doesn't show anything bad about me," Susan said.

"I'm sure it will not show anything bad about you. Besides, we're comparing the two, you to Sue, not looking at each genome individually compared to a standard."

"Okay, good." Susan smiled. "Are you staying here overnight?"

"I believe so," Ted replied. "I added enough rooms, I think, so a guest could stay here. Is that right?" He looked to David.

"Yes, we have the guest room ready for you," David replied.

Ted woke up to the sun. He expected to hear the sounds of the family getting ready, Sue for work and the kids for school. But the house was quiet. He took his time getting out of bed, and then walked down the hall to the kitchen.

ANDREW D. CARLSON

David was sitting at the table, quietly reading the newspaper and sipping his coffee. "Good morning," he whispered to his guest.

"Hello," Ted replied. He looked around. "Did I miss the scramble already? Is everyone gone?"

David chuckled. "It's spring break, no school this week."

"Ah."

"Sue slipped out this morning without disturbing anyone. She's good at that."

Ted smiled and nodded. "Yeah, I remember."

"Oh yeah, right," David said. "Sue *has* slipped out on you before. A couple of times, I think." He laughed quietly.

"Yeah," Ted replied with a sigh. "She did."

"Well there's no need for her to escape like that anymore. She just needs to go to work, that's all."

Ted nodded.

"Coffee?" David asked.

"Sure, thanks. And then I have to get dressed and head off to Manhattan."

David served Ted his coffee and shared sections of his paper. The two sat in silence for a while before Ted asked, "Has Sue or Brandy contacted the other clones from Europe?"

"Not that I know of," David replied. "I think they stopped when you told them to."

"Good."

The two continued reading.

Once he finished his coffee, Ted got up and went to the guest room and bathroom. He took a shower, got dressed, and packed his clothes. He walked into the kitchen. "Thank you, as always David, for your hospitality."

"Our pleasure."

"I will let you know the results of the DNA testing. I'll be in touch."

"Sounds good, Ted. Drive safely."

Ted nodded and walked out the door. He got in his car and drove off to Manhattan. On his way, he called Jim.

When Ted pulled in the driveway of the lab building, Jim was standing at the front door waiting. He opened the door as Ted walked up. "Welcome back, Ted."

"Good to see you, Jim. Today is results day. I'm excited to hear all about the data."

"Then come right in. The amigos are waiting in the conference room."

"Excellent." Ted followed Jim into the room.

Sarah, Cindy, and Bruno stood up when Ted entered. They all shook hands and exchanged greetings.

"Okay," Ted said, "whaddya got?"

"The samples marked 'c' are different than the others," Jim announced. "We four deduced that the 'c' was for clone."

"And we're assuming the 'K' was for Kansas," Sarah added. "The capital 'C' we guessed was for California, and the 'c2' was the baby clone."

"So much for coding," Ted said.

"Don't worry," Jim told Ted. "The four of us are the only people that know the codes. We logged the samples under long ID numbers, with no connection back to the codes you gave us. We memorized which ID number corresponded to the code you gave us. No one else knows."

"Okay, good," Ted replied. "Continue please."

"The differences we detected across the entire genome are the same as what we told you a few months ago," Jim said. "There are small substitutions, here and there, enough to change the proteins that are assembled from the DNA, but not enough to change the DNA fingerprints."

"These substitutions are actually very clever, if they were intentionally designed," Bruno said. "If the substance that triggered the cloning was the source for these substitutions, whoever sent it was pretty smart."

"Are you saying that the substitutions aren't random?" Ted asked.

"Well, we can't say for sure," Bruno replied, "but they don't appear to be random. If they were, there would probably have to be ten to a hundred times as many substitutions to result in the differences we've detected in the behavior of the clones."

"The cloned mice," Cindy clarified.

"Let me see if I got this straight," Ted said. He paused a moment to think. "We know the cloned mice have different phenotypes, right?"

The others nodded.

"We've tested them and know that cloned mice are smarter than normal mice, right?"

"Yep," Sarah replied.

"And we know that they can manage their metabolism better, right?" Ted continued. "And they can cool themselves better. And they have defenses against exposure to the sun, right?"

"Yes," Bruno and Cindy replied in unison.

"And these changes in phenotype definitely are a result of the goo that arrived on the planet."

The scientists nodded.

"So if we assume the humans have the same

phenotypic advantages, and we've tested their DNA, we know that these advantages are a result of a few small substitutions in their genome."

"You got it," Cindy said.

"Like I said," Bruno added, "whoever sent the goo knew what they were doing. And they were pretty smart about it."

"In what way?" Ted asked.

"They hid the changes," Bruno replied. "They didn't make the changes obvious. We had to look very closely, very deep into the genome to find the differences. They could have made substitutions all over the place, in big clumps of the genome, but that would have been obvious. The fingerprint tests would have flagged the clones as being obviously different. But instead, they hid the changes."

"Are you telling me that whoever sent the goo knew how to specifically modify the genome of humans on Earth?"

"It appears so," Bruno said.

"Or rather, they knew how to modify the DNA of all animals on Earth," Cindy added. "The mice had changes. I'm sure the other cloned mammals on the planet have the same advantages."

Ted sat in his chair, arms crossed, staring at the table. Eventually, he asked, "Are you saying that the alien species from the other planet that sent the goo knew the structure of the genetic material of the inhabitants of a random, distant planet? That seems way too convenient."

The team leaders frowned and stared at the table also. "You're right," Sarah said. "It's way too convenient."

Jim spoke up and told Ted, "Remember when

we talked about how the goo was sent here?"

Ted nodded.

"We said they probably blasted the goo all over the galaxy, hoping to hit a planet with intelligent people on it."

"Yeah," Ted agreed.

"So maybe they created several different versions of the goo, maybe hundreds or thousands, and the different versions were designed for different types of genetic material."

"Wait, how would they know what types of genetic material exist in the universe?" Cindy asked.

"They guessed," Jim suggested.

"Guessed?" Sarah said. "That would take forever to just randomly guess about genetic structure."

"Well, how long does it take for a planet to die?" Jim asked.

The others looked confused.

"They had a lot of time to work on it if they knew their planet was dying. It may have taken generations to randomly guess. Who knows, they probably had a lot more knowledge than us and knew about other possible genetic structures other than our DNA. They knew their planet was dying, so they knew they had to get their message out to someone, some other species in the galaxy. How else would they preserve the memory of their species?"

"Whoa," Cindy said quietly.

"Okay, this is pretty crazy to think about," Ted said. "I'm not sure we can even imagine what happened. I think we concluded last year that the extinct species got lucky, correct?"

The others nodded.

"Okay, we'll leave it at that. They got lucky.

And now we have clones all over the planet."

"All over the planet?" Cindy asked.

Ted sighed. "The clones have made contact with other clones around the world, mostly in Europe."

"Wow," Sarah said, "other clones. Cool."

"Not cool," Ted replied.

"Huh?" Cindy said.

"More clones will make my friends in Washington nervous. The idea of more of these 'aliens' will not please them."

"Ah, got it."

"So, tell me about the baby," Ted said. "What did her genome look like?"

"Well," Jim began, "we first ran a fingerprint to confirm she's the child of the other two. That turned out normal, just like we expected."

"Good."

"And when we looked at the specific clone sequences, we found the same changes, the same substitutions in the child as in the clone parent's sequence. The baby's sequence had mix of her parents, but when it came to the clone substitutions, her genome was the same as the other clones."

"So we know the substitutions continue in the next generation," Ted confirmed.

"Well, we only have the one sample, but yes, we think so," Jim replied.

"Okay, thanks. This is good," Ted said. He relaxed in his chair, leaning back. "Now, you will destroy any electronic data, correct?"

"We already have," Jim told him. "We did it last night, just the four of us, no one else was here."

"Good."

"Here is the notebook," Jim said, holding it out

for Ted to take.

"What's in it?" Ted asked.

"A summary of the results, high level. Basically, it just shows the sequences with highlighted differences."

"What will this tell me, or someone else who reads it?"

"It will just show that five DNA samples have five different sequences. Three have common specific differences, those are the highlighted sequences. The other two are random human DNA genomes."

"Speaking of which," Ted said, "do any of the non-'c' samples show any genetic anomalies or irregularities?"

"We don't know, Ted," Jim replied nervously. "You didn't ask us to look for any known mutations or irregularities."

"Good."

"Were we supposed to look?"

"Nope," Ted replied. "I just wanted to make sure you didn't." He smiled at Jim and stood up. He looked at the team leaders and said, "Thank you all. As usual, your contributions are monumental. It's a shame no one will ever know all that you do, but I'm sure that Jim, here, will be giving you extremely large bonuses this year." He looked to Jim and said, "Bill it to my account." He smiled and added, "Give yourself a raise while you're at it."

The scientists shook Ted's hand and they said goodbye. The team leaders walked down the hall to the labs, while Jim walked Ted out.

Just as they reached the door, Ted pulled out his phone and looked at it. "Shit."

"What is it?" Jim asked.

"I just got called to Washington."

Chapter 20 - A Matter of Time

"Welcome, Ted," General Gilmore said as Ted entered the room. Mr. Wright and Mr. Mason sat on either site of the committee chairman.

Ted took his seat and greeted the men.

"It's been a while since you gave a sit rep to this committee, Ted," the general announced. "We called you in to see if you had any updates."

"Nothing significant to report," Ted said calmly, sitting back in his chair.

"How are the ali… er, clones behaving? Any trouble?"

"Nothing to report."

"And the baby? How's the new baby behaving? Is she normal?"

"Well, I'm not sure if I can judge what's normal when it comes to babies, but she seems to be developing normally, maybe a little advanced for her age."

"What does that mean?" Mr. Mason asked.

"She seems more attentive," Ted replied, "you

know, more responsive than normal. I'd expect a baby this young to be rather dormant."

"And this baby is more responsive?" Mr. Mason confirmed.

"She seems to be," Ted said. "But that could just be my own impression. Maybe I'm giving her too much credit, thinking there's more than there really is."

"And what about the others, the children especially?" Mr. Wright asked Ted.

"They seem to be normal, no changes. They're all very smart."

"So you're telling us that there's nothing new to report?" General Gilmore asked.

Ted shook his head.

"Nothing at all? Everything is status quo?"

Ted shifted in his seat and then sat up. He nodded and replied, "Status quo."

General Gilmore looked left and then right at his fellow committee members. A smile appeared on his face. "How are the clones interacting in society? How do they fit in?"

"Uh... fine," Ted said hesitantly. "What do you mean exactly?"

"Do they do the normal things in society?" the general replied. "You know, Facebook and the like."

"Uh, I'm not sure about everyone," Ted said, "But the teenager in California seems to have a normal online presence. And she has friends in her high school."

"Any unusual activity?" Mr. Wright asked.

"Nothing unusual, not that I'm aware of."

The general grinned at Ted, no teeth showing, just a wide smile. "Well then, Ted, how do you explain all of these Twitter postings from the California girl?

They're with a girl in the Netherlands."

"Twitter is a global application. People tweet from all over the word. You know that. That's how the Arab Spring was reported to the rest of the world."

"True, but this seems to be a little more personal. The two talk about being clones, Ted. It seems that there is a clone in the Netherlands, Ted. Did you know about that?"

"I'm aware," Ted flatly replied.

"What do you think about that?" Mr. Mason asked.

"Um, I think it's interesting. If you stop and think about it, it's not unexpected that other clones arrived from the substance at the same time in other countries. The clones can't be assumed to be restricted only to the U.S."

"Sure, sure," Mr. Mason replied. "One other clone is okay, no big deal, right?"

Ted cocked his head at Mr. Mason and raised his eyebrow.

"There's at least twelve of them!" Mr. Mason shouted. "There are as many clones outside of the U.S as there are in the U.S.! And you think that's okay, totally expected, no worries?"

"It's expected. It's logical."

"It's an invasion!" the General shouted. "Just exactly when were you going to tell us?"

"It's not an invasion. It's just a couple young people tweeting with each other."

"They're all emailing each other, Ted!" the General bellowed, leaning forward, his face red with rage. "They're all sending each other emails in their crazy alien language!" He sat back, laughed, and continued, "They made it real easy for us to find them all. When will they learn to stay off the internet? Dumb, very dumb. Thankfully, we were able to hack the accounts and get the program so we could back-translate to English. It's only a matter of time, Ted, before we identify their plan."

"They are not planning anything. They're just greeting each other. That's it," Ted said.

"Oh really," Mr. Wright said. "And how can you be sure?"

"I know these people, the U.S. clones. They are not planning anything. It's not a terror threat or anything close to that. They're just saying hello."

"So you say," Mr. Mason said.

"So that's one thing you didn't tell us, Ted," the general said, more calmly. "Anything else?"

Ted sat silently in his seat.

The general got up from his seat and opened the door behind him. A short, young man entered the room and sat next to Mr. Mason.

"Do you know this man?" General Gilmore asked Ted.

"Uh, no, I've never seen him," Ted replied.

"This is John. He works for me," the general told Ted. "Most recently, he's been a laboratory technician."

Ted froze in his seat.

"He's been a temporary employee at Manhattan Laboratory Services." The general smiled. He held up a packet of papers and asked, "Have you seen these?"

"I don't know what those are," Ted replied.

"These are copies of laboratory notebook pages that contain the results of the genetic sequencing you had done on the clones."

Ted sat, stunned.

"You see, we had John, here, monitor activity at your friend's lab. Conveniently, he was hired to be a technician to work on your project. His grades from Kansas State were very high, perfect for this little temporary internship that the lab was offering."

"A fucking mole," Ted whispered.

"Yes," General Gilmore replied, "a mole." He smiled his wicked grin. "Now, I'm no scientist, but I'm pretty sure you had the genomes of the clones tested and compared them to their donors. And the baby was tested, too."

Ted shook his head slightly.

"Excellent work, I might add. And a great idea, Ted. This is perfect. John, here, tells me that there are differences. There's not enough to show up on a fingerprint test like you showed us a year ago," the general said. "Nice defense back then, by the way. 'Totally human, no difference,' you told us. I have to applaud you for that."

Ted's eyebrows lowered a little as he stared at the committee chairman.

"But the differences are detectable," General Gilmore continued, "and are specific to the clones. Thanks to you, Ted, we have a test to identify clones. John says it's time-consuming and expensive, not easy to run, but he says it's a definitive test."

Ted's face broke into a full scowl. His breathing became more rapid.

"You'll have to thank your friend, Jim, at the lab for the excellent work he did. Tell him to give himself and his team a big bonus for such excellent work." The general paused and grinned at Ted. He knew he had Ted cornered.

Ted sat silently.

"So, what are we going to do, Ted?" the general asked. "Any suggestions?"

Ted remained silent and still, staring at the General.

"Nothing? No suggestions?"

The room was silent

General Gilmore folded his arms and told Ted, "Don't worry, we'll take 'em all down. It's only a matter of time."

Ted folded his arms and glared at the committee.

"Can we count on you for your assistance, Ted?" Mr. Mason asked.

Ted didn't move.

"That's all for now, Ted," the general told him, brushing him away with his hand. "But keep your cell phone handy. We'll be calling."

ANDREW D. CARLSON

Chapter 21 - What's Done is Done

Outside, Ted pulled out his phone and made a call. "Jim, it's Ted. ... Not good, Jim, not good. ... It seems that your security wasn't as tight as you thought. ... A mole, Jim. You had a mole! ... They called him John. He was a short, little, greasy-haired rat with round glasses."

Ted walked to the street to hail a cab. He put Jim on the speaker of his phone. "How did he get in?" Ted hollered.

"He must have been one of the contractors."

"They said he had a fake degree from Kansas State. Anyone of your contracted employees come from Kansas State?"

"Jack! That little...! One of the interns was a guy named Jack, from Kansas State. He was shifty, always trying to stick his nose in our business," Jim told Ted. "He claimed he was just curious. He kept asking questions of the team leaders, but they didn't give him anything."

"He had copies of the notebook, Jim! How did

154

he get his hands on that?"

"I don't know, Ted. That notebook was always in our control. It was locked up when one of the four of us wasn't using it. The only way he couldn't have gotten it is if he broke into the lab."

"That must be how he did it. Look, this guy was no student. He was a professional. He was working for the committee."

"Jeez, I didn't even suspect he could be a mole. How stupid could I be?"

"Well, what's done is done."

"Yeah, but now what? What do we do?"

"There's nothing you can do. The results are in the hands of the committee. They have enough to take action."

"Action? What do you mean?"

"I'm not sure. They're going to do something."

"Against us?"

"No, not you, Jim. You and your lab are safe. You were only carrying out my instructions. You will probably get credit for uncovering the 'clone invasion' or whatever those bastards spin this into."

"But what about you?"

"I'll be okay. I have friends. It's the clones that I have to worry about. Something's going to happen. I just don't know what that will be."

"If there's anything I can do for you, Ted, just let me know. Anything. That includes the team leaders."

"For now, you should lay low. Just go about your business. Be a friend of the committee. Don't ally yourself with me. You were just following instructions, Jim. That's all you need to tell them. You were just following instructions."

"I feel awful. This is my fault. I let the mole get in and get out with the results."

"They were going to get it no matter what you did. If they had to arrest you all to get at those results, they probably would have. This way is much less painful, and you all still look good," Ted told him. "No, Jim, I screwed up. I got careless."

"We'll help any way we can," Jim said.

"I know. Thanks."

Ted ended the call and sat in the back seat of the cab, thinking. He sat silently until he reached his destination. He paid the driver and got out.

Standing on the sidewalk, he made another call. "Denise, this is Ted. ... No time for chit-chat. Listen, we're in trouble. I don't know how deep. But we're in trouble. The clones, us, friends, family, we're all in danger. ... The committee knows about the DNA testing. They had a mole in the lab. They know about the emails and the other clones around the world. ... I don't know, but we should be ready for anything. ... No more emails, Denise. You have to get Brandy to stop emailing people. ... No one. Not Sue, no one. They must stop. Now. Call the others and tell them. Tell David that something is going to happen. Tell Mary in Wisconsin. Tell Patsy, she's smart, she'll know what to do. Be prepared. ... I don't know. Make sure you have your phones charged at all times. Pack a travel bag for the baby, enough for a few days. Hide cell phones and chargers in the bag. Be ready. Tell the others to be ready. ... You've been through the drill when we first moved the clones. You know how the government thinks. Expect the same, only worse. ... I'm sorry, Denise, but things are no longer safe."

Chapter 22 - Be Ready

"Hello? ... Denise! How are you? How's-- ... Uh, okay, hold on. ... Alright, David's here and you're on the speaker."

"Are the kids close?" Denise asked.

"No."

"Okay, good. Listen carefully," Denise told them. "I just got a call from Ted. Something is wrong. He wouldn't tell me exactly what. I don't think he knows exactly what, but he's scared."

"Ted?" Sue asked.

"Yes, Ted," Denise replied. "He just called me and told me something is going to happen. The DHS committee he reports to knows about the DNA testing and they know about the email messages Brandy and you have been sending to the girl in the Netherlands and the man in Japan. They know about the clones around the world."

"So?"

"I don't know, Sue, but it's not good. I've never heard Ted this upset. He told us we need to prepare."

"For what?" David asked.

"He didn't know. He told me to expect something similar to before, when we first found the clones, when we took them to the base. He told me to pack a travel bag for Suzanne, one that will last for a few days."

"Okay…" Sue said.

"He also told me to hide cell phones and charging cords in the diaper bag."

"Smart," David said. "He probably expects that our cell phones will be confiscated, but he knows we're going to need to communicate."

"Should I hide all of them?" Denise asked.

"No," David replied. "We have to give up our phones. Everyone has cell phones, so they'll expect each of us to have one."

"What should I do?"

The line was quiet for a few moments. "Brandy's phone," David replied. "Hide Brandy's phone. We can tell whoever that she doesn't have one because you think she's too young for a phone."

"They won't believe her or me."

"But when she doesn't have one on her, they won't think to look elsewhere. They'll have to believe you."

"Okay."

"No matter what happens, we cannot fight," David said. "If we fight, they'll make life difficult. We have to cooperate, or at least appear to until we can assess the situation and make a plan."

"I'm scared, David," Denise said.

"Don't be. Just get things ready. Pack that bag. Think of anything that you need for the baby, and think of anything you can hide that might help us."

"Okay, I will."

"Juliana is smart. She'll know what to expect. She can help you get ready," David told Denise. "And Mary will know what to do. Janet and Larry won't be a problem. I'll call Patsy and get the Arizona folks ready."

"Do you think they'll do something to Richard?" Sue blurted out. "And what about Susan and Karen? And Petunia? They can't do anything with them, can they?"

"I don't know," David said. "But we need to be prepared for the worst."

"We'll get ready," Denise said. "And I'll call Mary. And all of us have to stop emailing right now, no more!"

"No more," Sue replied.

"Okay, stay close to the phone," Denise said. "Goodbye Sue, goodbye David."

Denise hung up the phone. Donald was standing behind her, Suzanne in his arms. Juliana was next to Donald. Brandy stood next to Juliana. Silence filled the apartment.

"You heard the conversation," Denise said. "We need to get a travel bag prepared. We need to fill it with diapers and formula. And we need to hide your phone, Brandy. We need to hide the charging cord, too. We need it to be ready at any time."

"Okay," Brandy replied. "Can I keep it until something happens?"

"No, we may not have time to hide it. You can

use your laptop."

"Mom!"

"There is no room for debate," Denise snapped. She took a deep breath and calmly said, "This is serious sweetie. We can't take chances."

"Okay."

"And you have to stop emailing the girl. You have to stop all communication. You'll put them in danger."

"How?"

"By knowing us."

"They're probably already in danger," Juliana said quietly.

The apartment fell quiet again.

After a few moments, Suzanne gurgled, breaking the silence in the room. Denise said, "I have to call Mary."

Brandy walked to her room. She found her charger, slowly coiled the cord, and then sat on her bed. She sighed. *Did I start this? Did I get everyone into this mess? Did it all start with posting the video? Are the others around the world in danger because of me?* She started to cry.

Suzanne quietly crawled into Brandy's room. She grabbed her sister's leg and said, "Dee-Dee."

Brandy smiled at her sister as she wiped the tears away. She picked Suzanne up and held her.

The baby reached for Brandy's phone and called out, "La-La." She held the phone up to Brandy.

Brandy smiled, first thinking it was cute. But as Suzanne continued to hold up the phone, she realized her sister was telling her what to do. "You're right!" Brandy said, sitting up straight. "I have to warn them!" She placed her sister on the floor and began tapping a new message on her phone.

@eline913 This is not a happy message. Be ready. Tell Lotta's parents and the others to be ready. I can no longer contact you.

Chapter 23 - Going Back

"I've texted with Ted every day, Sue," David told her. "Every day he responds. He doesn't know anything."

She folded her arms and frowned. "It's been two weeks! He's got to know something by now."

"Sue, he doesn't know anything. He's as much in the dark as us. He's one of us. He's not one of them anymore. He doesn't know anything."

"What are we supposed to do? Are we just supposed to sit here and wait?"

"Yes."

"This is unacceptable! We have to do something!"

"I understand it's your normal reaction to do something, Sue, but we can't. You cannot go anywhere or do anything out of the ordinary. You'll risk the safety of the kids, you, and me, maybe even the others."

"What am I supposed to do?" She stood in the kitchen, arms outstretched, palms up.

David stood up and walked over to her. He put

his arms around her and hugged her. He quietly told her, "Go to work. Do your job. Serve your customers. All will be okay. Nothing will happen to you, or to me, or the kids that will harm us. We're all strong. We're all together. We'll all be okay."

"But--"

"Relax, Sue. Just go to work. You have your cell phone. I can contact you if I need to. But nothing will happen. It will all be okay."

"I don't believe you."

"You have to. There's nothing else to do but go about your normal business."

Sue scowled at David or, more accurately, at the thought of not doing anything. She sighed and told him, "Give the kids a hug and a kiss from me before they go to school."

"I will."

Sue walked out the door. She emerged from the garage on her bike, and rode down the driveway to the road.

David sent a text message to Ted, asking if anything was different than the previous two weeks.

The sun rose and the kids woke to go to school. David fed them and made sure they had their homework, school books, and lunches. He hugged them and gave them each a kiss as they left the house to wait for the bus.

He watched as Karen met them at the bus stop, and he watched them until the bus arrived and they got on.

He spent the morning cleaning outside the house. The spring had brought warmth that allowed him to clean the gutters and rake up the few leaves that blew around the yard in the winter. He checked his phone frequently.

Sue texted him before the lunch rush, asking if there was any news from Ted. He replied.

> No response from Ted. But don't
> worry. That doesn't mean a thing.
> He's probably busy.

He sat at the kitchen table, thinking the same thing that Sue had. *It's not a good sign. Yes, he's busy. But he usually sends something.* He sighed. *Get a grip, David. It's okay. Everything is fine.*

David nervously fiddled around the house in the afternoon. He didn't accomplish a thing. He continued to check his phone for messages.

A car pulled in the driveway a little before three o'clock. David looked out the window at the black sedan. "Ted?" Behind the car, Sue rode up the driveway and into the garage. Behind Sue, a large white van pulled up. "That's not Ted," David said aloud.

Sue ran in the house. "They're here, David! They stopped me at work! They made me follow them home! They're here to take us!"

"Calm down, Sue, just calm down." He took hold of her arms and tried to settle her. "Tell me what they said."

"They told me to follow them home. They said they'd catch me if I tried to run."

"Is that it?"

"That's it."

"Nothing else?"

"No."

A man in a black suit walked to the front door and knocked. David opened the door for him. Sue hid behind David, looking over his shoulder.

"Mr. Hudson, Ms. Cook, you have fifteen minutes to prepare an overnight bag. Pack only the clothes you will need for you and your children, for two days. Do not pack anything else."

Sue started to argue, but the man silenced her by opening his suit coat and showing her his gun.

"May I come in?" he asked.

David knew there was no option. He couldn't refuse. He stood back, blocking Sue from reaching out at the man as he walked into their house.

"When your children arrive at the house, have them be quiet and stay on this level, in the kitchen. As soon as Ms. Clark, Ms. Roberts, and her daughter arrive here, we will be leaving."

Sue hollered, "You can't--"

"Ms. Cook," the man calmly spoke, "please don't make this more difficult than it needs to be. You are going to travel with us. Your family, Ms. Roberts, her daughter, and Ms. Clark will also travel with us."

"But--"

"Don't be naïve, Ms. Cook. You and I both know why we're here and why you're traveling with us today."

"No--"

"Silence," he hissed. "Discussion is over. Please take a seat before I'm forced to restrain you."

David took Sue's arm and led her to the table. They both sat and waited.

A little after three-fifteen, the sound of the bus made Sue jump in her seat. She was about to yell at the kids, when David grabbed her arm. "Don't," he sternly warned her, looking directly into her eyes. "They have to stay with us. If they run, they'll be in danger. They *need* to stay with *us*."

She tried to relax.

When the kids walked into the house, Sue leapt up from her seat and corralled them into the kitchen with her, shushing them from asking questions." Five minutes later, Petunia, Susan, and Karen walked in the door, escorted by another man in a black suit.

When everyone was standing in the kitchen, one of the men said, "We're loading up into the van. We're going for a short trip. Before we leave, please hand me your cell phones." He reached his hand out to David, Sue, Petunia, and then to Susan. "Do the kids have cell phones?"

"No," David confidently said. "They don't." David looked the man in the eyes without flinching.

The two men stared at each other for a few seconds. The other man finally blinked and said, "Good. It's time to go." He walked to the front door and held it open. The other man walked through, followed by the residents of Enterprise. "Lock the door," he instructed David, the last one out.

David locked the house and closed the garage door. He sat in the front seat of the van.

The two vehicles drove out of the driveway and onto the road. They continued driving, no one talking, until they reached Abilene.

The vehicles pulled into the airfield and directly into a hangar. Waiting for them was a white commercial jet with no markings. "Get on board," one of the men instructed.

David walked up the stairs first, followed by the kids. When he entered the plane, he saw Mary, Janet, and Larry sitting in seats toward the back. Behind them, Ted sat silently. David rushed to the back.

"Mary, Janet, Larry, are you alright?"

They stood and silently nodded.

"Ted," David said.

Ted didn't stand. He held his hands in the air. His wrists were bound together by handcuffs.

"What happened?"

"I didn't go quietly," Ted replied. He broke into a smile and chuckled. "I don't know what those ass holes expected, but I sure as hell wasn't going to go voluntarily."

David smiled at Ted. David knew that, although he appeared to be defeated, Ted was still going to fight. Ted was playing nicely for now, but David knew that wouldn't last for long.

Sue pushed her way past David, to the row in which Ted was sitting. "Ted!" she called out. "They handcuffed you!"

Ted calmly looked at her. "Yes they did, Sue. It was probably a good idea. I don't think I would have sat quietly. I'm sure I would have tried something. And they knew it, so... here we are."

"Where are they taking us?" Sue asked.

"I'm not entirely sure, but if I were to guess, I'd say we are going back to California."

"To Burbank?"

"Yes. But we'll only stay a few minutes, just long enough to pick up Denise, Donald, Juliana, Brandy, and the baby. Then, I'm afraid, Sue, we'll take off again and return to where it all started: the base."

Her eyes grew wide and she started to shake. "They're taking us back to the base?" she yelled.

"That's my guess," Ted calmly replied.

"They can't do that!"

"Oh, but they can, Sue."

David tried to calm her down. She shook his hands off her and leaned over the top of the seat to get close to Ted. "How can you just calmly sit there? We have to act! We have to stop the plane!"

"Go ahead and try," Ted responded. "But you will not be successful, and you'll only make it worse."

"Sue," David said. He pulled her back to the aisle and put his hands on her arms. "Now is not the time," he quietly told her. "We'll fight, but not now. Just wait until we get the others."

Mary, who had been observing the scene, stood and quietly told Sue, "You have the advantage. You know the base. We all do. They don't. We'll have the advantage when we get there."

Sue looked at Mary, processing what she said. "You're right, we do." She dropped her shoulders and relaxed.

"Let's go sit down and be with the kids," David suggested.

Sue nodded and turned to walk a few rows forward to where the kids were sitting with Susan and Petunia.

The plane took off, flying toward the sun. No one talked on the flight. When the plane landed, the door opened and three people got on.

"Patsy!" Sue called out, leaping into the aisle and running to hug her.

"Hi Sue," Patsy flatly replied.

"Richard," Sue said, as she hugged him.

"Hi Sue," he echoed.

"Martha," Sue said with a softer voice. "My best friend."

"Where are we going?"

"Back to the base. That's what Ted thinks."

"I don't want to go there."

"None of us do."

"What'll they do there?"

"I don't know. No one does. But Mary says we have the advantage. We know the base, we know the houses, they don't."

"What if they made changes?" Martha asked, looking at Sue.

"I don't know, Martha. I don't know." She hugged her friend.

One of the men in black barked out orders for the people to sit and buckle up. The plane took off again, heading further west, and landed after a forty-minute flight.

When the plane stopped next to a private hangar, the door opened and the rest of the group boarded. Denise carried the baby, followed by Brandy, Donald, and Juliana.

"Oh Denise," Sue called out.

"Ma-Ma!" Suzanne replied.

Sue let out a small laugh in response, but her smile quickly turned to a frown. She started to cry.

"Sue," Denise replied, as they met in the aisle.

"Su-Su!" the baby called out.

"That's right, Su-Su," Sue told her with a sad smile. "Don't forget you're Su-Su too, little girl."

The baby smiled and said, "Su-Su."

The man in black gave the passengers instructions and closed the door.

"Here we go," Sue called out to the group, "back to the base." She sat with her family and waited for the plane to land at its destination.

Chapter 24 - Enjoy Your Stay

In the fading light of the setting sun, the unmarked jet landed on the airstrip at the abandoned military base. It taxied to a stop. A mobile stairs vehicle pulled up, followed by two white vans.

The passengers were instructed to disembark by the man in black. As they walked down the stairs, they were met by silent soldiers dressed in fatigues and black boots. They were ushered into the vans and were driven to the base Exchange. Previously, it was the social center of the base, where the clones were able to choose clothes to wear, food to eat, books to read, and movies to watch.

The soldiers held the door of the Exchange open and motioned for the travelers to enter. As they walked in, they smelled the stale air inside, air that had probably remained inside over the many months since they were last there. The refrigerator and freezer stood in the front part of the building along with the now-empty shelves. Toward the back, the comfy chairs Ted bought for the clones sat covered in dust.

A soldier announced that food would soon be delivered. He instructed the travelers to be quiet and make themselves comfortable. He walked out of the Exchange, leaving the group alone.

"Now what?" Sue asked.

David immediately motioned for the group to get together in a group. They formed a circle in which they could talk.

"What do we have that we can use?"

"Not a thing," Larry replied.

"I don't have anything," Patsy said.

"We have Brandy's cell phone," Denise quietly said. "It's hidden in the diaper bag."

"Is it fully charged?" David asked.

"Yes," Denise whispered, "and we have the charger."

"Okay, good," David said. "What else?"

No one volunteered any additional items of use.

"C'mon guys," David said, "anything. Besides clothes, does anybody have anything?"

"Diapers," Denise said with a chuckle, "and formula. But I don't think those will be of much use."

"Under the right conditions," David told her, "baby formula is flammable."

Denise's eyes popped. "It is?"

David nodded. "And don't underestimate the repulsive power of a diaper full of poop."

Brandy burst out laughing. "Ha! Su-Su's poop is our secret weapon."

The others shushed her, but joined her in laughing, quietly, at the thought of soiled diapers as a weapon.

Ted stood off to the side, silently smiling.

"We can't do anything yet," David said. "Until

we know the entire situation, we need to get comfortable. We might be here a while."

The others dropped their heads, not liking the idea.

"We'll see what happens in the morning," David told them. "We can't do anything in the dark, so we should just settle in for now."

A car pulled up to the front of the Exchange, it's headlights shining inside. The group faced the front door and waited to see who would enter.

A tall, fat man dressed in fatigues and boots got walked inside the Exchange.

"Gilmore," Ted whispered.

"Who?" Sue asked, standing next to him.

"That man is General Gilmore. He is the chair of the committee."

"You mean the men who are responsible for us being here?" Sue asked excitedly.

"Yes," Ted replied. "I see he lost his suit in favor of fatigues, trying to look macho. What a total--"

"Ted!" the general called out from the entrance. "Welcome."

Ted simply sneered at the man.

"Commander," the general said to the man who had followed him inside, "I don't think Mr. Stevens requires those handcuffs. Can you please remove them?"

The commander walked over to Ted, through the group of people standing in front of him, and removed the handcuffs from Ted's wrists. The commander walked back to the front of the Exchange and stood just behind the general, off to one side.

"Welcome all," General Gilmore said with a smile. "I'd introduce you to each other, but you all know one another. I'd also show you around, but you already know your way around, so... Welcome back!"

Patsy swore at the general under her breath. "What an A-hole," she whispered.

"The Exchange here will serve as your barracks," the general continued. "Please, make yourselves comfortable." He looked back and motioned for the commander to step up, and then told the group, "Commander Wood will be in charge when I'm not here. Please follow his orders. And please do not try to overpower him and the others. I assure you we have enough strength and firepower to push you back. Let's all just get along, okay?" He paused, the grin still on his face.

No one moved, nor said a word.

"Good. Well, enjoy your stay," the general added. "I will leave you in the hands of Commander Wood." He turned and walked out the door.

"Lights out at twenty-two-hundred," the commander announced. "Make the preparations you need. Deliveries of food are being made. Do not interfere." He turned and walked out the door, leaving the group alone once more.

"There's nothing here," Sue complained. "What are we supposed to do? There's no books or movies. What do they expect from us?"

"They expect us to stay here," Ted replied. "They don't care what we do as long as we stay here."

"There's no coffee," Martha called out.

"There's no food," Patsy added.

On cue, a man wheeled in a cart of boxes. He was followed by the commander. The man went to the refrigerator and began filling it with essentials. He took gallons of milk, flats of eggs, blocks of butter and cheese, and packages of bacon from his cart and put them in. He placed jars of peanut butter and jelly, and loaves of bread on the shelves, along with bags of chips, stacks of plates, boxes of utensils, and rolls of paper towels. He unloaded four cases of water in bottles and placed them on the lower shelf. He then checked the boxes to confirm he had unloaded everything.

"Is that it?" Denise asked.

"That's all we get is bacon and eggs, and peanut butter and Jelly? What about something more healthy?" Juliana asked. "What about maybe some vegetables? And some turkey? How about some yogurt?"

The delivery man shrugged and shook his head. The commander said, "This will get you through the night and breakfast tomorrow. We'll delver more."

"Well make sure you get something more healthy," Juliana told him.

"And food for the children," Sue called out.

"And coffee," Martha added.

"And where are the books and movies?" Donald asked.

The commander stomped his boot and said, "I don't care how you all lived before. Now is different. Consider this a prison. No TV, no videos, no coffee. You're now residents of our prison, our prison for aliens, for global terrorists."

"Global terrorists?" Donald asked. "Is that what you think we are?"

"Anything that comes down to this planet and communicates in a language that no one else on the planet knows is considered a terrorist and hostile."

"What about us?" Denise asked. "We were born here. We can't write in the language. Why are we imprisoned here?"

"You're co-conspirators," he said plainly. "You knew all about the alien terrorists, yet you did nothing."

"There's nothing to do!" Denise yelled. "They're not planning anything!"

"Yes, of course," the commander replied. "Enjoy your stay." He turned and walked out.

The delivery man followed.

The group stood in place, stunned at the accusations the commander told them.

"Global terrorists?" Janet asked aloud. "How can we be global terrorists?"

"We're not," Larry said, putting his hand on her shoulder. "We're no terrorists, Jan."

They all started to disperse, some to the chairs, others to take care of the children.

"Can you give me a hand?" David asked Sue.

"Not yet," Ted told him. "I need to talk to Sue."

"I'll get started with the kids," David replied. He turned and walked away, leaving Ted and Sue standing alone.

Ted nudged Sue to walk toward the back of the building, into the unlit corner. He looked at her sternly, fire in his eyes. With almost a growl in his voice, he told her, "You got out of here before. Get us out of here now."

Chapter 25 - Have a Plan

Sue looked around. She found a door in the back wall. "Is that unlocked?"

"Only one way to find out," Ted replied.

They sneaked in the shadows to the door. Sue gently pushed down on the bar, waiting for resistance. The handle went all the way down and the lock clicked. She gently pushed on the door, hoping to not set off an alarm. There was no sound. She quickly sneaked out, followed closely by Ted.

They walked to the side of the building and spotted the delivery truck. They crouched and quickly walked to it, staying in the shadows.

The delivery man was distracted by the commander who was giving him orders for the following day.

Sue and Ted quietly climbed into the back of the open truck. They crawled to the back and hid behind a rack of empty shelves, out of the light.

Still listening to the commander, the delivery man threw the empty boxes into the back of the truck and hoisted his cart up and in. "Got it," he told the commander. He walked away from the door, to the cab.

"Search it!" the commander ordered the two soldiers as he walked away.

"Search it?" one soldier said to the other. "Why? The truck's empty. The dude just threw empty boxes in it."

"Yeah, well, we gotta check," the other said. "Orders are orders."

The first soldier turned on his flashlight and quickly waived the light to the empty boxes in the back, the boxes behind which Sue and Ted were hiding. "Close enough," the soldier told the other.

"Yep." The other soldier reached up and closed the door. A knock on the side of the truck was the signal to the driver that he was cleared to leave.

The truck started moving. Neither Ted nor Sue said a word. They drove for several minutes before Ted spoke. "That ought to be enough time to get clear of the base. C'mon." He moved to the door and waited for Sue to join him. "When the truck slows," he whispered, "we jump."

"What?" Sue whispered back, surprised. "We're going to jump?"

"Yes."

The truck eventually slowed to a stop. Ted opened the door and jumped. Sue followed behind. The truck pulled away from the intersection and continued on its route.

Ted started running away from the road, under the light of the full moon. Sue followed, and they ran along the dusty ground until they reached a small hill. They collapsed among the scrub-brush and cactus.

Once she caught her breath, Sue asked, "How is being in the middle of nowhere going to help us?" She rolled her eyes and shook her head at Ted. "At least I got to a truck stop."

Ted stood up, turned his back to Sue, and said, "Pull up my shirt."

"What?"

"Pull up my shirt."

Sue stood up and did as she was told.

"Do you see the phone taped to my back?"

"Yes."

"Pull it off."

She did.

He winced as she ripped the tape from his skin. He took the small, thin phone from her and held it up. "This is a special phone, untraceable. It was developed for the military to use in foreign countries."

"How is that going to help us out here?"

He tapped the phone and studied it for a few seconds. "Okay, got the coordinates." He dialed a number and waited for an answer. "Kermit, this is Paddington. Sending coordinates now."

"Roger Paddington," the voice on the other end replied. After a pause, it said, "Route confirmed. ETA is twenty-one forty-seven."

Ted looked at his watch. "Roger. Paddington out."

"What is going on?" Sue cried out.

"Did you think I would allow myself to be taken prisoner without having an escape plan?"

"Um…"

"Well, I have a plan," he said with a smile.

"What is it?"

It's about nine fifteen right now. In about a

half hour, at nine forty-seven, you and I will be picked up by a helicopter."

"A helicopter? How?"

"Ever since I met with the committee and found out about the mole, the spy they had at the lab, I knew I was in trouble. I knew we were all in trouble, including your new friends around the world. I knew the committee was going to do something. I figured it would involve containment."

She cocked her head and frowned at Ted.

"It's what I did to you all when you first arrived, before we knew anything about you. You all were 'contained' on the base. Until we knew about you, we had to keep you separate from everyone else."

"So now the government is doing the same thing?"

"Yes, but they don't care about learning more about you or the other clones. They have only one thing on their minds."

"We're not getting off the base, are we?"

"Well, you and I did. And now we have to convince others to let the rest go. If not, we're all going to be there for a long time, including you and me."

"How are we going to convince others?"

"I have friends. We need to convince them."

"And they're the ones who are picking us up?"

"Yes."

"How did you do all this?"

"I've been around a while, Sue. I've learned a few things, just like you. Most importantly, I learned that I always need to have a plan."

"Like this?

"Exactly. You see, I've never trusted the committee. They put military men on it. I don't think any of them have any science knowledge at all. And yet, they were assigned to oversee the investigation of a strange foreign substance by the Chemical and Biological Division, my division. Wouldn't you think the oversight committee would have a science background?"

"Yes, I guess."

"Ah, but they don't. They only have one thing in mind, assess and eliminate any threats to the United States."

"Are we a threat?"

"You were, or at least a potential threat, when you were first cloned. Think about it, a strange substance appears on the planet and all of a sudden there are more mammals on the planet. And then new humans appear! Of course they had to consider it a threat."

"But you proved we were human."

"Exactly. And that should have been the end of the committee. They should have been disbanded. But they weren't. The department still considers you a threat."

"But we're not."

"You know that and I know that. But they don't want to believe it."

"Why not?"

"Some people don't understand science. They're scared about anything they don't know."

"And they run the country?"

"Some people are in positions of leadership, yes. Thankfully there are people who do understand science."

"Your friends, the ones that are picking us up, right?"

"Yes."

After a few minutes of silently sitting in the desert, Sue asked, "All those people in government, aren't they all elected?"

Ted laughed. "Well, the president is. And the members of congress are, but that's it. The Supreme Court is nominated. Cabinet members are nominated. And the rest, all of the people that assist and advise the president and members of congress are all hired, just like regular jobs. And in Washington, those jobs are given to friends. Those people aren't elected, they're selected. And there are hundreds, if not thousands of times as many people. Those are the people that influence how things get done in Washington."

"You mean that the elected people aren't in control?"

Ted laughed again at her naiveté. "No. They're more like puppets."

"What?"

"Puppets, you know, with strings tied to their hands and feet. Elected officials do and say what their selected friends want them to do and say."

"Really?"

"Unfortunately, that's how it works, Sue. It's not a perfect system. But it's worked for nearly two hundred and fifty years."

"Huh."

"Listen, while we're waiting, I need to briefly tell you the results of the DNA testing," Ted said.

"I know. David told me. My DNA is different from Susan's DNA. I thought we were clones, exact copies."

"You and she are close. But not exact. And the differences in your DNA are what make you a clone.

The differences, the substitutions in your DNA, are also in Donald's DNA. And Suzanne has the same differences."

"So these substitutions are the same for the clones? So I match Donald more than Susan?"

"No, the differences are very small between you and Susan. But those differences that the lab detected are the exact same as with Donald's and Suzanne's DNA. Think of the small differences as markers for clones."

"Something to look for when testing a person to see if they're a clone or not," Sue confirmed.

Ted sighed and nodded.

As Sue continued to digest what Ted told her, a faint thumping sound began in the distance. "That's us," Ted said.

"What?"

"Can you hear it? It's the helicopter."

"That tapping noise?"

Ted stood up. "Just wait. It'll get a lot louder."

And it did. The approaching noise grew in intensity until Sue felt the thumping of the rotor blades in her chest.

Ted flashed a light from his phone into the air, signaling the helicopter of their position.

The dust of the high desert started swirling around them and flew into the air. Sue followed Ted and covered her eyes and face from the blowing sand.

The helicopter landed, but didn't slow its rotors. The noise was deafening. Ted stooped and started walking. Sue followed. They approached the side door. It slid open for them and they got on board.

Ted took a pair of headphones from the wall behind him. He motioned to Sue to do the same. He put them on and waited for her to put her pair on. "Are you okay?" he asked her.

She nodded.

Another voice sounded in their ears. "Welcome aboard Paddington. ETA to rendezvous base is twenty eight minutes."

"Roger."

The helicopter lifted off.

Chapter 26 - We Can't Just Sit Here

"Mom's gone," Kati cried. She sat in front of David, cross-legged and sobbing.

David wiped the sleep from his eyes and sat up. He looked at Kati, and at the other kids sitting just behind her. Violet and Tyler were softly crying. Zachary had tears in his eyes. "Sue is not gone," David calmly told them. "She has not escaped. Well, not like before."

"Yes she has!" Kati blurted out, wiping the tears from her eyes.

He patted the air and whispered, "Okay, you're right. He looked into Kati's eyes and said, "But she's safe. She's with Ted."

The kids instinctively looked around the room, trying to verify if Ted was inside.

"They're on a mission," David continued quietly, looking into the eyes of each child. "Kinda like a spy. I don't know what she's doing, but Ted has a plan."

"Are they coming back?" Violet asked.

"I don't know," David replied. "They're going to do something outside of this base. I hope they come back. I hope they come back with a lot of other people that can help all of us get out of here."

"So do I," Zachary whispered. "I hope they bring back the Special Forces or the SEALs."

David quietly chuckled. "I don't know about that, son."

"Mom will get help, I know it," Violet added.

"Are you sure?" Kati asked.

David nodded at the children and said, "She'll get help. She and Ted will, somehow."

"Are they gonna be in trouble for escaping?" Tyler asked.

"I don't know. I hope not. But I don't know for sure."

Susan woke up and instinctively looked for her daughter. She found Karen sitting with the other kids, talking to David.

When Karen saw she was awake, she told her mother, "Sue's gone."

Susan looked to David for confirmation. He nodded.

"But she's safe," Karen added. "She's with Ted. They're gonna get help, we think."

David nodded again.

Brandy came over and sat with the other kids, rubbing her eyes. "Hi," she croaked.

"Hi," Violet replied flatly. "Sue's gone," she said, as if it was expected.

Brandy nodded. "I noticed last night that she wasn't here."

"But she's with Ted, so it's okay," Violet added.

Brandy nodded.

185

Donald and Denise joined the group, carrying Suzanne. The baby was wide awake and gurgling. Denise sat on the floor and let Suzanne crawl among the others. She looked to David and asked, "Sue?"

David shook his head.

Denise nodded.

"But she's safe," Brandy added. "She's with Ted."

David said, "Hey, listen." He made eye contact with all of the kids before continuing. "Those guards out there, the ones that are watching us, they don't know that Sue and Ted are missing. Do you understand?" He waited until all of the kids nodded in agreement. "So you all have to be quiet and not say anything, okay?" Again, he waited for the kids to acknowledge. "You cannot say anything about them not being here. Don't even talk about them, okay? Don't say the name Ted, and don't say the name Sue."

"Su-Su!" the baby called out.

Everyone looked at the baby.

Soon, the others joined the group and they all sat in a big circle, the adults surrounding the children. "We need to think about feeding all of us," Juliana said.

"I'm not that hungry," Brandy said. Her mother agreed, and the others began to nod.

"We're not hungry now," Juliana replied, "but we will be soon, especially the kids. And I assume that some of us have to go to the bathroom."

They all nodded at the last comment.

"I'll go find out if any of the houses still have functioning kitchens and bathrooms," Juliana told the others. "We left everything in good condition, but I'm not sure they'll be working after a year and a half."

"I'll come with you," Brandy offered. "Can I?"

she asked her mother.

Denise nodded.

"Let's go, lil' sis." Juliana stood up and Brandy joined her.

"I think a man should go with them," Larry said. "They'll have to deal with them soldiers."

"Actually," David replied, "women, especially young women, are less threatening to soldiers. Those two will have a better chance than you or I. The soldiers don't know yet who the leader of this group is. I'm not sure I even know, now that Sue and Ted aren't here, but they will expect the leader to be the most threatening. They expect the leader to try to lead an escape. And they probably expect a man to be the leader. So the girls are perfect to ask about cooking and bathrooms. The soldiers won't think they're up to something. They're just being domestic."

"That's so stereotypical," Patsy said.

"Trust me," David replied. "It's how the military works. And we need to remember that while we're here. We need to take advantage of that." He motioned for Juliana and Brandy to go.

The girls walked to the front of the Exchange and out the front door.

"What are you doing?" one of the guards barked. "Get back inside."

"We have to go to the bathroom," Juliana said. You stuck us in a building with no bathroom. We all have to pee."

"Where do you plan to pee out here? In the grass?" the soldier asked. He and his partner began laughing.

Juliana dropped her shoulders and silently stared at the soldiers until they stopped laughing. "See those houses right there," she said, pointing across the street. "Those used to work. They used to have functioning plumbing and electrical. We're going to go across the street and see if they still work." She began walking. Brandy followed.

"Um…" was all the soldiers could say. They looked at each other, shrugged, and let the girls go.

"This was Sue's house," Brandy said as they approached the first house.

"Let's see what works," Juliana said. She opened the door and cautiously walked inside, holding the door open for Brandy.

The kitchen was dusty, but there were no bad smells. Juliana lit the stove. Brandy opened the oven and the light came on. "This works," she said.

"Good," Juliana replied. She walked to the sink and turned on the faucet. Dirty water splattered out, followed by air. Eventually, the air was pushed out and clean water started flowing. "Okay," she said. "Go flush the toilet," she told Brandy. "You'll probably have to flush it several times."

Brandy walked to the bathroom and flushed the toilet. It shuttered with a loud bang, causing her to jump. She tried two more times no water flowing. She turned on the faucet at the sink and it spit out air, like in the kitchen, but it soon flowed with clear water. She flushed the toilet again and water began to flow there too. "We're good here," she called out as she walked back to the kitchen.

"Okay, good. We have one functioning house," Juliana said. "Should we check the other houses?"

"At least one or two more."

The girls exited the house and started walking to the next house. They heard the guards yell something. "We're checking another house!" Juliana yelled back as she and Brandy continued walking.

They repeated the same steps in two more houses, checking the electricity and stove, and flushing the water lines to have operating sinks and toilets.

"After flushing all this water," Juliana said, "I've got to pee." She laughed.

"So do I," Brandy replied. "You first."

Brandy waited for Juliana, and Juliana waited for Brandy, and then the two girls left the house. "C'mon, we better go get the others and tell them the bathrooms work." They jogged back to the Exchange.

When they reached the front door, they told the guards that the pluming worked, so the others would probably come out to go to the bathroom.

The guards didn't say anything. They just watched the girls go back inside.

Soon after, David and Susan exited the building with the five smaller children.

"Hey!" one of the soldiers yelled. "One at a time!"

David stayed silent. Susan boldly said, "I think we can walk these kids across the street so they can go to the bathroom. I don't think that should be a problem." She nudged Karen and Kati forward to walk across the street. The older kids followed and David brought up the rear.

They broke into groups, the guys went into one house, the ladies went into another. When they were all finished, they walked back to the Exchange. Kati and Karen skipped and hopped along the way. They were in much better moods after using the bathroom.

The rest of the group continued the journey to the houses, a few at a time to not upset the guards.

When Mary walked back to the Exchange, she thanked the guards and walked inside. The rest of the people were standing in a group. "I'm hungry," Tyler called out. The other kids agreed.

"Okay, let's get cooking," Juliana called out. "Who's on toast duty?

Between the adults, they figured out who would make the eggs and who would toast the bread. They assigned Donald and Richard as runners to deliver the plates of food back to the Exchange from the houses.

By late morning, everyone was fed and in much better moods. The adults sat in the comfy chairs while the kids sat on the floor, playing with Suzanne, the only source of entertainment.

"What are we going to do?" Janet asked the others. "We can't just sit here, can we?"

"We don't have much choice," Juliana replied.

Denise whispered, "We do have a cell phone," she told the others, patting the diaper bag sitting on her lap.

"Yeah, but who are we going to call?" Patsy asked. "It's not like there's anyone out there who knows we're here."

"Sue and Ted," Larry quietly said.

"But we have no idea where they are. We don't know if they have a phone and we certainly don't know the number," Juliana whispered.

"What else can we do with a phone?" David asked the others, prompting them to think.

The others sat, thinking. Patsy whispered, "Do we still have the internet here?" She looked at Denise and Juliana.

Juliana shrugged and Denise shook her head.

"Okay, let's hope the soldiers turned on the

internet. We can use the phone to tweet or post on Facebook," Patsy said. "Who has accounts?"

The adults looked at each other. "I have one," Martha replied. "But I never use it."

Janet and Larry shook their heads, as did Mary. Denise and Donald shook their heads. David did too.

"Okay, so it's just me and Richard," Patsy replied.

"I have a Twitter account," Juliana replied.

"Okay, that's three," Patsy said. "How many followers do you have?" she asked Juliana.

"I don't know," she replied, "maybe a couple hundred."

"I don't have many either," Richard said.

"Guys," David said. "You're missing one very important, very connected person."

"Ted?" Richard asked.

David looked to the kids on the floor. "Brandy."

Denise called, "Brandy, can you come here for a minute?"

Brandy stood and walked over to her mother. The other adults leaned in to listen.

"We have your cell phone. If you were to send out messages, tweets, Facebook posts, those kind of things, how many people will see it?"

"It depends," Brandy replied. "I don't have thousands of followers, but if I use hashtags I can tweet to everyone. I just don't know how many people will see the tweets."

"What would we even say?" Patsy asked. "Help us, we're trapped?"

"Good point," David said. "We have to think carefully about what we want to say."

As they sat and quietly thought, the silence was broken by the roar of jet engines from a plane landing on the airstrip."

Chapter 27 - You'll Get Your Chance

"Where are we going?" Sue asked. She and Ted rode in the back of a black sedan.

"We're going to the residence of the Secretary of the Interior," Ted replied. "Do you remember him? He was the gentleman who met us at the school in Burbank last year."

"Charles, the man who traveled with the First Lady, right?"

"That's the guy."

"What are we going to do at his house? Have lunch? I don't think we're dressed for a nice lunch." She wiped and patted the desert dust from her clothes. "We're still a little dirty from last night."

"As a member of the President's cabinet, the Secretary has some influence. Remember that the President is the Commander in Chief of the military. Chuck, my friend, the secretary, is going to call in the General and his minions for a little conversation."

"Minions?"

"Mr. Mason and Mr. Wright, the other

members of the committee."

"Those are the men that put us back at the base, aren't they?"

"Yes, those are the men."

"I hate them," Sue replied, her eyebrows dropping into a scowl.

Ted chuckled at Sue. "They're not too fond of you, either."

"They've ruined our lives."

"They're trying to, Sue. But something tells me that you all won't let that happen. You'll do something. You'll adapt, find a way to move on and prevail."

"Prevail?"

"Win."

The sedan pulled up to a brownstone condo in a wealthy neighborhood. "This is his house?" Sue asked. "It's doesn't look like a house."

"This is what houses look like in Washington. They don't have quite as much land to build big houses as you do in Kansas."

The two got out of the car and walked to the door of one of the residences. A man opened the door. "Ted! I'm so glad to see you. And Sue! It's nice to see you, too. C'mon inside."

"Hi Chuck," Ted said.

"I see you made it out," the secretary said. "Everything go alright?"

"Like clockwork," Ted replied. "We're a little tired and dirty, but that will work to our advantage."

"How are you, Sue?" the secretary asked. "Are you okay?"

"Just a little dirty, Mr. Secretary."

"Please, call me Chuck."

"Okay, Chuck."

"Do you remember me?" he asked. "I sure remember you and the others. I was proud to be part of the 'clean up the planet' campaign you all started."

"Thank you, Chuck," she replied. "And yes, I remember you, too. I'm honored to be here with you."

"I hope you brought your boxing gloves."

"Boxing gloves?" Sue asked.

"I'm just the promoter," the secretary replied. "I just arranged to get you and Ted in the ring with the other three."

Sue gave Ted a confused look.

"Boxing," Ted told her, "is a sport where two people punch each other until one knocks the other down."

Her eyes popped. "We're going to punch each other?"

Ted laughed. "No, just verbal punching. You and I are going to talk to the committee members."

"I got my money on you two," the secretary said. "You'll knock 'em out for sure."

Sue looked from the Secretary to Ted. "I thought you brought me along just to escape. I didn't know I'd be fighting."

"We're not going to be physically fighting. But we are going to be telling the committee members exactly what we think about their decision to contain all of you, and the others from around the world."

"They have the others?" Sue called out excitedly. Her fists clenched at the end of her rigid arms. "They went and got Eline and Aki and everyone else?"

Ted placed his hands on Sue's arms to calm her down. "Yes, by now the other clones from around the world are at the base, along with anyone that knows them. If they're not there yet, they're on their way."

"Oh! Those...! Let me at 'em! I'll strangle them!"

The secretary laughed. "Ring the bell now. She's ready!"

Ted laughed at his friend's comment and Sue's reaction, but he still tried to calm her down. "I have no doubt you'll tell them what you think, Sue. But relax. You'll get your chance to voice your opinion."

Sue stood tense, ready to fight.

Ted turned to the secretary and said, "Let's review the plan."

"Okay, but first, let's sit down and get comfortable." He led the others to chairs in a sitting room. There were three lounging chairs and three hard, upright chairs from the dining room. "We'll sit here," the secretary said, pointing to the lounging chairs. They sat and relaxed.

"First, I'll question them why a Director of DHS, my close, personal friend, has been fired," the secretary told Ted. "The general will know that it's not really my business to ask, but he knows that the President and I are close, so he'll start talking. Besides, you know he hates to be challenged, so he'll go on the defense right away. That'll be your chance to go after him and the others."

"It won't be easy to convince them."

"That's why you have your secret weapon," the secretary said, pointing to Sue. "You didn't bring her along just to look good. This will be the first time those bastards will come face-to-face with a clone. *We* know she's human, but they still think she's some sort of alien. They're still afraid of her. Just let Sue loose and see how it goes."

Ted laughed. He looked at Sue and said, "They have no idea what we're about to unleash on them."

The secretary laughed.

"But what if it doesn't work?" Sue asked. "What if we can't convince them to let us all go?"

"If you can't convince them, it might be over," the secretary said.

"No," Ted replied, "it'll be time for Plan B."

The doorbell rang. The secretary stood up and said to the others, "Wait here quietly." He walked to the front entry and opened the door.

"What the hell are you playing, Chuck?" a gruff voice, the General's voice, asked.

"It's Mr. Secretary, if you please, General, and you're here for a little conversation. Please come in."

The sound of several shoes on the floor told Ted and Sue that all three committee members were there.

"Mr. Mason, Mr. Wright, welcome to my house."

They didn't respond.

"Please let's go in here and sit." The Secretary led the others into the room.

When the general came into view, he saw Ted and froze. "How did you...?"

The secretary sat in the last lounging chair and pointed to the dining chairs. "Please, gentlemen, sit."

The general slowly took a seat, looking at Ted, and then at the woman in the room. The others sat in the remaining dining chairs.

"General, you've met Ted before, of course." The secretary pointed to Sue and told the general, "This is Sue."

The general's eyes popped ever so slightly.

"I thought we could start our conversation by having you and your committee members justify why a Director of Homeland Security, my personal friend here, was fired from his position. What exactly are the reasons for his termination?"

"I don't believe that we have to answer your question, Mr. Secretary," the general snapped, crossing his arms. "That's a matter of internal DHS affairs."

"I understand," the secretary responded, "but Ted is my friend. I'm personally concerned."

The general didn't move.

"And the President will likely question the move. He and I are close, also. And the President knows I'm Ted's friend, so the question will probably come up at some point. I thought I might ask you to help me give an answer to the President."

"I don't have to answer anything," the general snapped.

The secretary simply sat in his chair, legs crossed, hand folded in his lap, calmly waiting for an acceptable response."

The general didn't budge.

Neither did the secretary.

Sue looked from one to the other and back again, seeing who would give in.

The secretary calmly looked at his watch. "You know, I believe that we have an *ad hoc* cabinet meeting this evening. I'll probably have a few minutes to privately talk to the President."

"He's a traitor," the general blurted out, pointing to Ted. "He's conspired with the aliens and their plot of global terrorism. He and the aliens, and anyone connected with them have been contained, for national security."

"Aliens? Global Terrorism? Plot? What plot?" the secretary asked, shocked at the accusations.

"Classified." He crossed his arms again.

"Oh really," the secretary replied. "I seem to have a pretty high security clearance. I don't suppose you'll tell me the details."

The general sat silently.

"Well," the secretary continued, "assuming you followed proper protocol, I can get those reports from the security council. I can certainly ask the President to ask for the details, when I see him this evening."

The general shifted in his chair.

"Anything?" The secretary asked.

"The aliens are being contained for the safety of the nation and the world. The aliens continue to pose a threat."

"How?" Sue called out. "How are we a threat to the country? How are we a threat to the world?" She leapt up from her seat. "You know nothing about us!"

The general looked at Sue, eyes darting, unsure of what she would do. Mr. Mason and Mr. Wright were startled, and sat uneasily in their uncomfortable chairs.

Ted smiled as he sat, watching the men.

"And we're not aliens!" Sue yelled. "We're humans! You have our DNA, you know exactly what we are. We're human. We're not from another planet. We were cloned here, on Earth, from other people." She started to pace the floor.

The committee members followed her movements with their eyes.

"Yes, the substance that we were cloned from arrived from another planet. But we're human. We've had two tests now that prove we're human."

She walked to the general and stood in front of him. "If you had paid enough attention to the DNA tests, you'd know there are differences. But those differences are no greater than the differences between you and me. The substance made some changes compared to my other person, the Sue I was cloned from. But those differences are no threat. Yet you seem to think they are. I bet if we compared my DNA to yours, we'd find differences, substitutions, mutations, and flaws that would make you different from me, from everyone else. Should we lock you up?"

The general sat silently.

Sue resumed her pacing back and forth. "My DNA is different from people of other races, from other countries and continents. But we're all still human, aren't we? Should we lock up anyone with different DNA? And who's DNA would be the one against which everyone else's DNA would be compared? Is it your DNA?" she asked, pointing at Mr. Wright. "Is it yours?" she asked Mr. Mason. "No, it's got to be the general's DNA, doesn't it? He's the one that decides who gets locked up. So anyone who has different DNA from the general gets locked up!"

The general sat up and said, "You--"

"Don't say anything!" Sue snapped.

The general shrank in his chair.

"Should we lock up humans who have different skin color than yours? What about short people? What about those who are bald? They have different DNA. Should they be locked up? You think the answer to everything is to lock up anyone that you don't understand. I can tell you, Mr. General, that none of us are going to cause harm! We are not terrorists! Locking us up on a military base is not the answer.

We're free people! People! Not aliens! Not animals! People!"

The general raised a finger to talk.

Sue stomped her foot on the floor. "I'm not finished yet!" She backed away from the general and looked to each of the committee members. "The differences that make us clones are differences designed to *help* people of the Earth. We have advantages that will help all humans adapt to the changing Earth. It's evolution! We're not a threat! We're here to help!"

Sue breathed heavily, catching her breath as she stood in front of the men.

"Are you finished?" the general asked.

Sue nodded.

Slowly, the general stood up. "It seems that this alien has said all that she needs to. And since she has no evidence that she and her alien friends are here to help, I see no reason to change my mind. Since she and her friends have conspired against the United States of America, using coded messages, repeatedly violating the law over the past year, I see no reason to release her and her co-conspirators. They will be made to stand trial."

"Didn't you hear a word I said?" Sue protested.

The general laughed to himself and shook his head. He walked over to Ted and motioned for him to stand. The general frisked Ted, all over his body. He found the cell phone tucked into Ted's sock. "Nice try," he told Ted with a grin. He frisked Sue, and then told the two, "We're going back to the base. Don't even think about trying to escape again."

The secretary asked his friend, "Plan B?"

Ted smiled and replied, "It's already in effect."

Chapter 28 - We're All Friends

The group stood up and walked to the front of the Exchange to look out the windows and see what was happening. The sound of the plane meant someone or some people were at the base. *Is it the General? Are Sue and Ted back? Maybe that plane is going to take us back home.*

Shortly after, they got their answer. Three white vans pull up to the Exchange. But the vans were not empty. The heads of many people could be seen inside all three.

David quickly instructed the group to stay together. "We need to stand together as a group and hide the fact that Sue and Ted are gone."

"Shouldn't we spread out?" Patsy asked.

"We need to make it look like we're all together, so they don't go searching the building. If they count us, we're in trouble. But if they see all of us together, in a group, we may be able to convince them we're all here.

"Who is it?" Janet asked.

"I don't know," David tersely replied, keeping an eye on the activity outside.

Guards approached the vans and opened the doors. The people inside slowly climbed out and stood by the vans, waiting for instructions.

David made a quick count. "There's around thirty people there, maybe one or two less."

Brandy, standing near the front of the group quietly called out, "Eline!"

"What?" Denise said.

"It's Eline!" Brandy whispered. "These are the clones from all over the world!"

"Are you sure?"

"Positive!"

"It makes sense," David said. "If they're going to contain us, they have to round up the others from around the world, the ones you've been emailing."

"But there's too many," Brandy said. "There are only fourteen clones."

"They must have family and people that know about them," Richard said.

"There's only twelve of us clones," Donald replied, "but there's, like, twenty of us here."

The group inside the Exchange silently waited for the others to enter.

Commander Wood led the others inside the building, talking slowly in basic English. "You will be here, in this building," he said pointing around the ceiling. "You will stay with these people from the United States," he continued, pointing then to the clump of people standing deeper in the building. "They will explain to you," he said, waving at the newcomers, "how to live here. Enjoy your stay."

He and the other soldiers walked out of the

Exchange.

The newcomers stood, looking at the U.S. group. They were silent and scared. For a few moments, no one in the building moved.

Brandy finally stepped forward, looking to one side of the other group, and asked, "Eline?"

A tall, blonde-haired girl stepped forward and replied, "Brandy?"

"Yes!" Brandy replied. She ran to her friend.

Eline met her halfway, and the two hugged. They stepped back and Eline wiped her eyes. "We are so frightened," Eline said.

"Don't be. It's okay, we're all friends," Brandy said. She hugged Eline again. The two parted and Brandy told her, "It is so good to meet you. C'mon, let me introduce you."

The U.S group instinctively thinned out to more of a line. Brandy walked down the line, introducing each person. She finally got to her family. "This is Donald, he's sort of my dad. He's a clone, like me."

"Hello, Donald," Eline said as she shook his hand.

"This is Juliana. She is not a clone. She's more like my aunt, or a big sister. She's part of my family."

"Hello, Juliana."

"It's nice to meet you, Eline."

"This is my mom," Brandy told Eline.

"I am so happy to meet you," Eline said.

Brandy took the baby from her mother and showed her to Eline. "And this is Suzanne."

"Su-Su!" the others called out, laughing.

The baby smiled, gurgled, and echoed the others, "Su-Su!"

Eline laughed at the baby. "She is so beautiful!"

Brandy blushed as she held her sister. Eline looked at the others, reviewing who she just met. "You are without someone," Eline told Brandy, looking confused. "Where is Sue?"

"Uh, well…"

Denise stepped forward and said, "It's a little difficult to explain right now. We'll tell you later, okay?"

Eline hesitantly nodded, knowing something wasn't as it should be. "Okay," she replied.

"Can we meet your friends and family?" Denise asked her.

"Yes, of course," Eline said with a smile.

The U.S. group slowly followed Eline and approached the new arrivals. They spent the next half-hour meeting one another, the nineteen Americans each greeted the twenty-six people from around the world.

When Brandy and Eline came to the other family from the Netherlands, Brandy held Suzanne up to see them. She told her sister, "Suzanne, this is Lotta."

Suzanne looked at Lotta, smiled, and then called out, "La-La!"

Lotta looked back at Suzanne, smiled, and replied, "Zu-Zu!"

The two older girls laughed with each other. "They should play together," Eline said.

"Good idea," Brandy replied. She turned and started walking toward Denise.

Eline talked to the Dutch family and they all followed Brandy. Brandy handed Suzanne to her mother and told her the babies should play together. Denise found a spot for the babies to crawl around.

The larger group broke into smaller groups,

mixing people from different countries. The groups then broke apart and coalesced into different groups, each person getting to know one another.

While everyone talked in the Exchange, a delivery truck pulled up. Two delivery men brought in additional supplies.

Toward the back, Eline pulled Brandy aside and said, "We cannot stay here."

"I know," Brandy replied. "Before you arrived, we were talking about what to do." She leaned close to her friend and whispered, "I have a cell phone."

"So do I," Eline replied. "I told them I was too young to have one. I cried when they didn't believe me. They believed me then."

"You're smart," Brandy replied. "So what should we do?"

"We have to make a connection with people outside of here."

"But who would we contact? Everyone that I know, anyone that can help us, is here."

"The same is for me. And the government isn't going to help us."

"So all we can do is send out tweets and post pictures on Instagram."

"But what will we say? Please come and help us? No one can just come here to get us, can they?"

Brandy shook her head. She sighed. "I guess we just tell people that we're here."

"Where is here?"

"We're in California. We're at an old military base. It's not close to my home in Burbank or Los Angeles, but we're still in California."

"Okay, let's start tweeting to our followers that we're being held in California. Maybe we can bring attention to us."

"Okay," Brandy replied. "Let me get my cell phone." She walked over to where the babies were playing and picked up the diaper bag. She looked around for guards before digging through the diapers and formula to find her phone. She set the bag down and carried her phone to the back corner of the Exchange. Eline followed her.

Brandy took out her phone and powered it up. While she did that, Eline took her phone from the rear waistband of her pants.

Brandy's phone beeped and buzzed as it connected. She tapped and scrolled, looking at the various notifications, and then her eyes widened. She froze. "It's from Ted."

"Who?"

"Ted. He's our leader," Brandy whispered. "He escaped with Sue. That's why Sue isn't here. They escaped to find help. Ted is in the government but he is our friend. He's not like the soldiers outside."

"What did he say?"

"He sent a text message. It says, 'This is Ted. I know I told you to delete the video you uploaded in November. But now I want you and the others to make many videos. Upload them to YouTube. Tell everyone that you're clones. Tell them how and why you arrived.' "

Chapter 29 - The Message

"A message from Ted?" Denise asked. "How? When did he send it?"

"Um, lets' see." Brandy found the date stamp on the message. "Five-thirty this morning. We were sleeping."

Denise waved David over. When he reached them, Denise whispered, "Ted sent a text message to Brandy at five-thirty this morning."

David scratched his chin, his eyes darted back and forth. "That means he has a cell phone. And it's probably secure. And... he probably didn't send the text at five-thirty his time, so he's east of here, probably two or three time zones. Which means... he's probably in Washington, D.C.," he concluded. "That's gotta be it. He and Sue somehow made it to Washington."

"They're safe?" Brandy asked.

David nodded.

"Why would they go to Washington? To talk with the committee?" Denise asked.

He laughed. "No, definitely not... I don't

think." He cocked his head in doubt. "He's probably made contact with someone who can help. Let's just hope he was successful."

"So what about the message?" Denise asked. "Should we follow it?"

"Let me read it." He held Brandy's phone and read Ted's message. "Absolutely. These are pretty clear instructions."

"Okay," Denise replied. She looked at Brandy and said, "Go for it. Start making videos."

Brandy and Eline both broke into smiles.

"But don't let the guards see you," David warned. "If they see the phone, they'll confiscate it, and that will be it. Those soldiers," he said pointing to the front of the building, "cannot know we have a cell phone."

"Two cell phones," Eline told him. She smiled.

"You hid a cell phone?" David asked.

Eline nodded.

"Smart. That was very smart," David told her with a smile. "Ask others if they have phones. But quietly ask. Use as many phones as you can to make as many videos as possible."

The girls nodded and started to walk off.

"But don't get caught," David quietly reminded them.

Brandy and Eline casually walked from person to person, asking each if they had a cell phone. No one did. But when they reached Aki and asked, he smiled at them. "You do?" Brandy whispered.

Aki nodded.

"How did you do it?" Eline asked.

"I know how government think. Everyone in Japan have cell phone. So I have two. I hide one in my waist of jeans. They find that phone." He smiled. "I hid other phone in my sock." He looked around the building to confirm no guard was watching before he lifted his leg and pulled a small cell phone from his sock.

Brandy's eyes grew wide when she saw the phone. "Can you take video with that?" she asked.

"Yes, photo and video."

Eline told him, "We have been told by the man that is friends with the American clones to post videos about us to YouTube."

"We will be caught," Aki replied.

"Yes," Brandy said, "but if we all quickly post enough videos online, too many people will see them. If enough people learn about us, they will try to help. Ted, the man who's our friend, hopes that the right people, his friends here in America, will see the videos and help."

"That is good idea. How do I help?"

"Talk to the other Japanese clones. Post videos in Japanese and English."

"My English is not good."

Eline smiled. "It's okay. We just need people around the world to see the videos. I will have the others make videos in their own language and in English."

"I don't know another language," Brandy quietly said. "I'm learning Spanish, but I can only speak English."

"It's okay," Eline told her with a smile. "Many people around the world speak English. This will work."

"What do we say?" Brandy asked. "Ted told me to say that we're clones. He told me to say how and why we arrived, but does that mean we tell them about the slimerge?"

"Yes," Eline replied. "We tell them people touched the... what did you call it, 'goo'? Yes, we tell them people touched the goo and we were cloned from it. We tell them we're copies."

"But we have to make sure we say that we are human. We have been tested. Our DNA has been tested and we are human."

"You said that your friend Ted told you to say why we arrived," Eline said. "Why did we arrive?"

"Do you know about the message?" Brandy asked. "Did you clones in Europe feel the message?"

Eline looked at Brandy and slowly whispered, "Do you mean about the other species from the other planet?"

"Yes!" Brandy excitedly whispered back. "It's okay to admit you received a message. We all did. It's from the extinct species--"

"From the dead planet," Eline responded.

"Yes! You got the message too! That's why we arrived. The substance, the goo, was sent to Earth as a memory of the extinct species. And that substance cloned people so we could deliver the message. We need to clean up the planet. We need to save Earth before we die like they did."

"The other clones in the Netherlands had the same idea inside their brains, like me. We didn't know if it was a dream or if it was a real memory. But we all had it."

"We get same dream!" Aki told the girls. "The Japanese clones had idea of extinct species from other planet."

"Yes!" Brandy replied to both. "That's why

we're here! We're here to deliver the message about the planet. The goo cloned us to carry the memory of the extinct species, so we all save our own planet."

"How did you know the dream had that message?" Eline asked.

"I think Sue was the one who figured it out. But it took a while to really understand it."

"That is amazing," Eline said.

"Very amazing," Aki echoed.

"Okay!" Brandy said excitedly, but quietly. "Let's make some videos!"

"We need same title in video," Aki told her.

"Yes, we need everyone to know that the videos are connected, so they can search YouTube for other videos from us," Eline said.

"What should we use?" Brandy asked.

"I like the word 'goo'. It sounds funny," Eline said, laughing.

"How you spell 'goo'?" Aki asked.

"Gee, oh, oh," Brandy replied.

"Goo clone?" Aki asked.

"That doesn't sound good," Eline replied. "What about 'clones from goo'? Is that good?"

"I got it: 'Cloned from goo'." Brandy typed it on her phone for the others to see.

"That's good," Eline told her.

"I like," Aki replied. "Cloned from goo."

Slowly, over the rest of the afternoon, Brandy, Eline, and Aki walked among the others and explained the idea of using videos to share the clone message and asked them to film themselves, always watching the guards to make sure they didn't see.

By dinner time, over thirty videos were uploaded to YouTube. The three Japanese men each made two videos, one in Japanese and one in English. The clones from Sweden, Belgium, and France each made videos in their own languages, as well as English. The two clones from the UK made one video each in English, as did the American clones. Eline made several videos, including one with Lotta, who gurgled and babbled throughout.

When Brandy saw Eline and Lotta, she picked up Suzanne and asked her mother to film her. Suzanne did as Lotta, gurgling throughout. She even called out "Su-Su!" when Brandy said her name.

Finally, Eline suggested to Brandy, "Let's film the two babies together. We can hold them."

"Great idea! We can have the mothers film us."

The girls sat on the floor next to each other, holding the babies. The mothers filmed the scene while the rest of the people blocked them from the view of the guards outside.

The older girls each introduced themselves first, and then introduced the babies. When Eline said Lotta's name, Suzanne called out "La-La!"

When Brandy said Suzanne's name, Lotta called out "Zu-Zu!"

The two babies gurgled together.

When Eline and Brandy mentioned the substance, both babies laughed. "Zu-Zu goo," Lotta said, giggling.

"La-La goo," Suzanne replied, pointing at her friend.

The older girls stopped talking and watched the younger girls interact. In their laps, the two babies started conversing. "Dee-Dee goo," Suzanne said, patting her older sister.

"Leena goo," Lotta replied, looking up at Eline.

"Da-Da goo," Suzanne continued.

"Da-Da goo, Ma-Ma goo," Lotta called out.

The others in the room stood silently, watching the two babies talking to each other. Eline and Brandy were stunned.

Lotta crawled out from Eline's arms and pulled herself up using the older girl's shirt. She looked over to Suzanne and said, "Zu-Zu."

Seeing her playmate, Suzanne did the same. She flopped on the ground and crawled to the side of Brandy. She pulled herself up and proudly stood tall. "Su-Su!" she called out with a smile.

The others in the room broke into laughter at what they saw.

"You're still filming, right?" Brandy asked her mom. Eline asked the same in Dutch. Both camera-women nodded.

Lotta and Suzanne both laughed and cackled with glee.

Chapter 30 - Help Us

As Brandy and Eline uploaded the last of the videos, the roar of jet engines filled the Exchange.

"Someone's here," David announced.

"Who could it be?" Martha asked.

"No idea," David replied.

"Maybe it's an empty plane to take us home," Janet said.

Larry laughed at her. "We'd all like that, Jan, but I don't think that's gonna happen. We're still prisoners."

"Maybe Ted was successful," Janet countered. "Maybe he sent the plane to take us home."

"There's still the problem of them soldiers, don't ya know," Larry said.

"Oh, yeah," Janet replied.

"Well, whoever it is, I hope they're friendly," Martha said. "I don't like how things are going so far."

"We'll find out soon," David said.

The people in the exchange moved to the front to see who was arriving. They waited for a few minutes before a single white van pulled up to the building. A soldier got out of the front passenger seat and opened the rear door. He helped out the first passenger.

"Mommy!" Kati called out.

"She's handcuffed!" Violet added, shocked.

The group stood in silence as they looked at Sue. She was expressionless, waiting for instructions from the soldier.

The soldier helped the second passenger out of the van.

"Ted," Zachary and Tyler said in unison.

"At least they're together," David noted.

The soldier walked the two prisoners to the front door. Before opening it, he took their handcuffs off.

When Sue and Ted walked inside, the others crowded around them to hear their story. Ted put his hands up and asked for silence. "Let's all calmly walk to the back," he told them slowly and quietly. "Pretend that everything is fine. Don't huddle like we're planning anything. Just pretend we came back from the bathroom."

The prisoners in the Exchange started to walk in different directions, trying to be as nonchalant as possible. They broke into groups and pretended to have conversations while they all walked toward the back of the building, away from the windows.

Ted and Sue took seats in the comfy chairs. David and the kids took seats on either side of them. The kids welcomed their mother back, while Ted and David de-briefed.

"You obviously weren't successful," David said.

"Not true," Ted calmly replied. "We made it to Washington. I made contact with friends. We even had a pleasant conversation with the committee."

David's eyes grew wide. "You did?"

"Well, Sue did most of the talking," Ted replied. "She had an impact. She said what needed to be said."

"Then it probably wasn't a very pleasant conversation," David deduced.

"I enjoyed it," Ted said with a smile. "She rattled those men pretty well. I think Mr. Mason and Mr. Wright were ready to cave. Unfortunately, our friend, the general, wasn't. He's still convinced the clones are about to attack the planet and everything holy that he stands for."

"So we're right back where we started?" David asked.

"Far from it," Ted replied happily. "The secretary made it very clear that he'd be talking to the President. He put the general on alert. But that bastard is so cocky that he underestimates his situation. When a cabinet member talks to the Commander in Chief, it's no trivial matter."

"So we're good then."

"Eh, not exactly," Ted replied. "The general may ultimately report to the President, but he, too, has friends that are helping him to pull this off. So, it might not be easily undone."

"So…"

"We put Plan B into effect."

"Plan B?"

Ted sat up, nervous. "Didn't Brandy get my text? Please tell me you made videos and posted them to YouTube."

"Oh, that. Yeah, we did that. They made a lot, all of the clones. The others from Europe and Japan made videos in multiple languages."

"Good."

"So what's next?   What's the plan?" David asked.

"We wait," Ted said, sitting back in his chair.

"For what?"

"For things to percolate."

Brandy walked over to the chairs. She stood in front of Ted and quietly told him, "I got your message. I did what you asked me to do."

"David mentioned that you did.   Excellent," Ted said with a smile. "You did a great job, Brandy. I hear that everyone pitched in and made videos, in multiple languages even."

Brandy nodded and smiled.

"I knew I could count on you."

She beamed with pride. "Eline helped me," she told Ted, "and Aki."

"Well, I must thank them. Can you take me to them so I can meet and thank them?"

"Sure! Follow me."

Ted stood up.   "Before we go," Ted told Brandy, "I think we need to take Sue with us.   She needs to meet the others."

Ted held out his hand for Sue. She paused the conversation with her kids, took Ted's hand, and stood up. She, Ted, and Brandy went off to find Eline and Aki.

"May I have your attention," the general's voice boomed throughout the Exchange. "Everyone, please move forward and stand here in front of us. Now.

The group did at it was told. Susan and Sue

corralled the girls, while David herded the boys to the front. Lotta's mother carried her, while Denise carried Suzanne. The swarm of people slowly arrived at the front and stood in a long line in front of the general, Commander Wood, and two soldiers.

"You are all aware that Mr. Stevens and Ms. Cook have been returned. And I hope you noticed that they were handcuffed." He paused to look up and down the line of his detainees. "I want to make it clear to you all that any further attempts to escape will be dealt with in the most severe way." Again, he paused. "I have instructed Commander Wood to have his men shoot anyone that is out of place."

The group rustled.

"You will stay in this building. You will not be moved to houses. You will only be allowed to leave to use the bathroom or to prepare food And you will then be escorted by soldiers. There are no other instances for which you will be allowed to leave the building."

"What about the children? They need to--"

"Silence!" the general bellowed. "There is no room for discussion, Ms. Cook. After your latest experience, I think you should be glad you're not more tightly confined."

Sue glared at the general, her eyes piercing his.

"You will stay here, in this building, until your next destinations are readied, where you will all be arraigned and stand trial."

"Trial?" David blurted out. "For what crime?"

"I guess you'll find out at your arraignment, won't you Mr. Hudson?" He turned to leave and nodded at the commander.

The commander and the soldiers stood still until the general got into his vehicle and drove off.

Seeing the general gone, they backed toward the door and exited, always watching the prisoners.

"That ass hole!" Sue yelled.

"Mommy! You said a bad word," Kati informed her.

"Yes I did, sweetie," Sue replied, still staring out the front window. "I most definitely said a bad word at a very bad man."

"Now what?" Patsy called out.

"We wait," Ted said.

"For what?" Denise asked.

"Something to happen," Ted replied.

"What?" Donald asked.

"I don't know," Ted said.

The group stood silently, not moving.

"Sue," Ted finally said, "I think you have a video to make, don't you?"

"I do," she replied. "Let's go make that video." She took the young girls' hands and said, "Brandy? Will you help me?"

"Sure," Brandy replied. "I'd be glad to."

"In fact," Sue called out, "I think everyone should help out. If the general and his soldiers want us to stay here in this building, that's just what we'll do. He didn't say we couldn't make a video or two. He didn't say that we couldn't all hold hands and protest. So let's go."

She led the way toward the back of the Exchange, her daughter's hands in hers. Brandy joined her, followed by Denise and Suzanne. David and the boys fell in behind, as did Donald and Juliana. Soon, the entire group walked purposefully, following their leader.

"Who will shoot the video?" Sue asked. "Who

has cell phones?"

Brandy, Eline, and Aki raised their hands.

"Okay, good. We need to shoot this with as many phones as possible. We need every chance to get the word out."

The three with cell phones stood back, waiting to film Sue.

"No wait," Sue said. "You three are the reason we all came together. You have to be in this video."

"But who will take the video?" Brandy asked.

"I can do it," David volunteered.

"No, you have to be in the video with me."

"I can," Donald said.

"No, you're a clone. You have to be in it too, and Suzanne and Denise. In fact, all of you have to be in this video. We all have to stand together."

Mary stepped forward. "I can film the video on one phone. I don't need to be in the video."

"Okay, but I feel bad," Sue replied.

"Please, don't," Mary said. "Someone has to take the video, otherwise you won't deliver your statement to the world. No one will see you or hear your voice."

Two other people, friends of two European clones, stepped forward and also volunteered.

"Thank you," Sue told them. "Okay," she told the rest, "get together in a group. Children, you stand in front, while the adults will stand in back. The world has to be able to see everyone's faces."

The group arranged themselves into a large pack. The three camera-persons stepped back to be able to see everyone.

"Ready?" Sue asked.

The camera-people nodded.

"Okay, three, two, one…

"My name is Sue. And these people around me are my family and my friends. We're all together, being held against our will by the U.S. government. Why are we being held against our will? Why are we *prisoners*? You, see, some of us are clones.

"A clone is a copy of another person. I am a clone of Susan. She's standing here next to me. You can see that we look like each other. How was I cloned? Susan touched a substance that was on the ground, a substance that was delivered to Earth. We call it goo. Susan touched the goo and I appeared. There are others who touched the goo and made clones. There are eleven clones from the goo in the U.S. There are thirteen clones from the goo in other countries around the world. There are even two babies who were born from clone parents.

"So who are we? We're human beings, people, the same as you. We had our DNA tested. We have the same DNA as everyone else on the planet. We clones also have some differences. But those differences don't make us non-human. People from Japan are still human, but they have differences in their DNA compared to people from America. And women have differences in their DNA from men, but they're still human. And people with different skin color or different hair color have different DNA. But we're all human, aren't we? Yes, including us, the clones.

"What do we want? Why are we here? The substance that arrived on the Earth, the same substance that we were cloned from, contained memories of an extinct species from a dead planet somewhere in the galaxy. The extinct species sent the substance to other planets in the hope that they would be remembered.

We, the clones, carry that memory and are sharing it with as many people as we can. Our family and friends, all of the people around me, know about the extinct species. And now you do.

"I bet you think that's it. But it's not. You see, the clones have special adaptations. We can control our appetite and our weight. We can control how much food and water we need. We can control our body temperature. We have special adaptations that will help us to survive on a warming planet. And we can pass those adaptations on to future generations. We can help save the people of Earth. Through evolution, we can help the people of Earth survive a warming planet. We can help save the people of Earth from extinction.

"But we are not being allowed to do that. You see, all of us here are currently being held as *prisoners*. The U.S. government and the military are holding us as prisoners on a military base in California. They are going to put us on trial for terrorism. *Terrorism*! We clones, and even our family and friends who *aren't* clones, are going to be tried as terrorists! Why? Because we talk to each other. Because we share our message with the world! That's it! We live free and talk to each other. That's it. *How is that terrorism*?

"We just want to help the people of this planet. We may be different, but we're people too. We have as much right to live our lives and help to make this planet better for our children, and their children, and future generations. But the government believes that is terrorism. And they're going to lock us away forever because they don't understand. They don't believe in evolution. They probably don't even believe that the planet is warming. So twenty six people who talk to each other are standing up for what we believe, and that makes us terrorists. They're afraid of us, so they lock us away. *Forever!*

"Share this video with people you know. Tell as many people as you can that you saw this video. Tell everyone that you think it's unfair that we're being held here. Tell everyone you know that you don't think we should be *prisoners* for just wanting to live and help. Tell people they should let us go. Tell people we should be able to live our lives, as *free people*. Help us spread the word. Help us, please."

Chapter 31 - Something Has To Happen

"So how many views do we have so far?" Sue asked Brandy. "Are people seeing our videos?"

"Yeah," Brandy replied. "I don't know how many as of today, though. Let me check." She tapped and swiped her phone. "Most of our videos have... a lot of them have hundreds of views so far."

"That's good, right?" Sue confirmed.

"Yeah, that's pretty good," Brandy replied. "We can't tell who's looked at them, but that many views in a couple days is pretty good." She continued looking at her phone. "Oh, wow!"

"What?"

"Your video, Sue, you know, the one with all of us in it and you talking, it's got close to ten thousand hits!"

"Really?"

"Yeah. Your video is by far the most popular," Brandy said, "although, the one with Lotta and Suzanne has a lot of views too."

"Let's tell everyone. C'mon," Sue said, walking

toward Ted and David. Brandy followed.

"Hey Ted," Sue quietly said when she approached him. "Brandy says that our videos each have hundreds of views. The video with all of us has ten thousand views."

"Excellent," Ted replied. To Brandy he said, "I assume that many views is a lot by YouTube standards, correct?"

"Yeah, that's a lot. I mean, some videos get millions of views if they go viral, but, like, ten thousand is a lot."

"I hope that's enough," Sue said.

"Hey," Brandy timidly said, "Why aren't we using the phones to do more? We've been sitting here for two day, waiting for something to happen. Why don't we call someone?"

"I'm sure that just about everyone is listening to your phone lines," Ted replied.

Brandy cocked her head and frowned.

"By now, the CIA or military has hacked into your phones. From the videos, I'm sure they figured out the specific frequencies of your phone, and the phone companies probably helped them. So they'll be listening to any calls you make, you and Eline and Aki."

"Can they do that?" Sue asked.

"Sure, why not? They can do just about anything they want," Ted replied.

"Isn't that illegal? Don't they need a warrant?" David asked.

"I'm not sure these days," Ted replied. "It seems the CIA can do just about anything, all in the name of fighting terrorism. Whether it's legal or not, I guarantee someone is listening. They can't stop us from using the phones for the internet, or they haven't stopped us yet, but if we try to call someone, they'll intercept the call."

"Oh," Brandy flatly said.

"So what are we going to do?" Sue asked. "We can't just sit here waiting."

"That's exactly what we have to do." Ted replied.

"But it's been two days! *Something* has to happen. If no one is going to get us out of here, *we* have to do it ourselves," Sue argued.

"I don't think forty-some-odd people can sneak off the base in a truck," Ted said. "We would not be successful. And that would only make our captors angrier. They're going to be pretty pissed as it is when they discover we posted videos to the internet."

Right on cue, General Gilmore burst into the Exchange. "What the hell has been going on in here?" he bellowed.

Commander Wood, who had followed the general inside barked out, "Prisoners, front and center, now!"

Everyone slowly got up and walked to the front of the building. They stood together in a group, David and Ted in front, the parents shielding the children from the two men and their guards.

"I found out that you aliens have been making videos!" the general continued yelling. "Well, isn't that special? Some of you snuck in cell phones. Who was it? How did you do it?"

No one in the group moved, some out of defiance, others out of fear.

"Well? Who was it?"

"It was me," Ted said, stepping forward.

"Bullshit, Ted. You were thoroughly searched

when we brought you back."

I will take full responsibility," Ted told him proudly.

"I know you will," the general replied with his evil grin. "But I still need to know who snuck the phones in." He stood, looking from person to person in front of him. "Don't make me search you all. It will be much easier if you come forward on your own."

The general and his men waited. After a few moments, the general gave a slight nod to the commander. He snapped his fingers the two guards started to walk forward.

"Okay!" Brandy screamed. "Here, take it." She walked past her mother and Donald, past David and Sue, and past Ted. She held the phone out for one of the guards.

The guard snatched it from her hand and she ran back to the middle of the group. The others closed around her, protecting her.

General Gilmore looked at the phone after the guard handed it to him, slowly studying it, silently. The wicked smile grew on his face. He dropped the phone to the ground and violently stomped on it. He picked up the crushed device and threw it against the nearest wall. It shattered into pieces.

"There are two more phones," the general calmly called out. "I would like them to be brought forward."

Eline and Aki slowly walked forward. Neither of them wanted to get too close to the soldiers, so they tossed their phones at the general's feet.

"Thank you," the general politely said before stomping the phones into pieces.

He stood up, adjusted his uniform, and took a

deep breath before continuing. "Now, I have some good news for you all. I have expedited the arraignments of the aliens for several crimes against the United States. I won't go into details. You'll find out tomorrow," he said, smiling. "So, we have twenty six aliens who will stand trial."

Both Sue and Denise pushed to the front of the group and protested. "You cannot put the children on trial!" Sue yelled.

"They had nothing to do with this!" Denise shouted. "You cannot do anything to the children!"

"Oh, really?" the general replied. He paused for a second, and then admitted, "You are correct, Mrs. Jackson. We cannot try the children."

Sue and Denise both lowered their shoulders and sighed.

"The children will not be put on trial because, as you said, they didn't do anything. But Brandy did," he said, grinning.

Denise lunged at the general, screaming. Ted and David managed to reach out and restrain her before she got close to the soldiers. They held on to her tightly and pulled her back to the group. David looked to Sue and told her, "Don't even think about it."

Sue didn't reply. She simply stood and stared at the general, breathing heavily, rage in her eyes. She was poised to charge.

"So there are a few less clones than I originally said," the general calmly, proudly told the group. "Only those that exchanged encrypted emails will be charged with crimes against the state."

He paused to let the group consider his accusations. "Commander," he said, "please restrain the accused."

"Don't you dare!" Sue called out. "We will not stand trial for living free! We will not stand trial for being who we are!"

The commander first approached Sue, holding on tightly to keep her from attacking the general. The two soldiers stood between her and the general, hands on their guns.

"You are mistaken, Ms. Cook," the general calmly told her. "You will stand trial."

The commander turned Sue around and tied her wrists with a zip-tie. He walked her over to the side wall and told her to sit.

He moved next to Donald and repeated the same activity. When he approached Brandy, Denise broke down and sobbed.

"It'll be okay Mom," Brandy said.

Denise collapsed to the ground crying.

The commander tied the wrists of Martha, Patsy, Janet, and Larry, and moved them to the wall. He then pulled Aki and the other Japanese men from group and tied them up. He did the same with the European clones. Eline's parents cried, but after seeing the guards react to Denise, they chose not to fight.

When the commander stood in front of the remaining three clones, Lotta, her mother, and father, he turned to the general and said, "Sir?"

"You have your orders," the general tersely replied. He brushed his hand, instructing the commander to continue.

"You cannot take that baby from her parents!" Denise yelled.

"I can and I will," the general forcefully said.

Denise ran to the family. The mother handed Lotta to her. Denise wrapped her arms around the baby, protecting her from the commander and the soldiers. Lotta's mother nodded at Denise, tears running down her cheeks.

Denise stepped back and stood next to Juliana who was holding Suzanne. Neither baby was gurgling. Silence filled the room.

The commander bound the wrists of the remaining clones and sat them against the wall with the others.

"Don't forget him," the general called out. He pointed at Ted. "We cannot forget the leader of these alien terrorists now, can we?"

David made a move to protest, but Ted waved his hand and shook his head. He did not resist.

After the commander finished, he and the soldiers walked back and stood behind the general.

"Okay," the general said. "That does it for now. We'll see you in the morning. Have a pleasant evening." He gave his prisoners one last smile before turning and walking out.

The building was full of silence. No one said a word. They either stood or sat, not wanting to believe what happened or what was about to happen.

Finally, Sue broke into tears. "All we've ever wanted to do was be free!" she sobbed. "All we want to do is help. Why can't they understand that?"

Seeing Sue sit on the floor, crying in desperation, Kati and Violet started to cry. They ran over to Sue and kneeled on the ground. They hugged their mother and sobbed with her.

The other kids started to cry and joined the detainees at the wall. Soon after, the rest of the group moved to the wall. Everyone was kneeling or sitting. Everyone was crying.

Chapter 32 - Someone's Coming

As the sky started to fade from night into dawn, Ted stirred. He looked at the others, and then at the ceiling. "David," he whispered, trying to nudge him with his arms, still tied behind him.

He scooted a few inches on the floor to be closer. "David," he quietly said, pushing on him.

"David woke up and looked around, surveying the scene. He looked at Ted.

"Do you hear that?" Ted asked.

"Hear what?"

"Listen." He waited for David to detect the sound.

"Helicopter?" David confirmed.

Ted nodded. "Someone's coming." He twisted onto his knees. "C'mon. We gotta get everyone up."

"For what?"

"For whoever is in that helicopter." Ted got to his feet and tried to stretch his body.

David started to move. Sue was leaning on his shoulder, and she, too, started to move. "What?" Sue asked, groggy from sleep.

"We need to get up," David whispered. "Someone's coming."

"Who?"

"I don't know?"

"How do you know?"

"Listen," David instructed.

Sue stopped moving and looked up. "Helicopter?"

"Yes."

"Who?"

David shrugged, and then stood. He helped Sue up and started telling the children to wake up.

Soon, the entire group was awake. The unbound people helped those who were tied. As they stretched, the thumping of the helicopter grew louder.

"Who is it?" Larry asked Ted. Everyone looked to Ted for his response.

"I don't know," Ted replied. "It's either someone good or someone bad."

The group moved to the front windows, looking for the source of the noise.

As they stood there, a car and two military vehicles pulled up to the front of the Exchange. The general leapt out of the car and the commander got out of one vehicle, followed by soldiers.

But instead of entering the Exchange, they looked to the sky and then to each other. The general began yelling at the commander and the soldiers.

Inside the building, no one could hear what they were saying, but Ted smiled. "They're pissed," he told the others. "That helicopter is not one of theirs."

The thumping rattled the roof of the Exchange, and then a marine helicopter appeared just above the building. The tail twisted around and the helicopter landed on the street.

"C'mon," Ted boldly said. "We're going outside." He walked to the door and threw his body against the handle on the door. It flew open.

Ted emerged from the building followed by everyone else. The general and soldiers didn't even notice. They were too busy looking at the helicopter.

The jet engines powered down and the rotors began to slow. The noise faded and the dust began to settle.

Everyone waited to see who would emerge.

When the rotors stopped, the door opened. The Secretary of the Interior stepped out.

"Chuck!" Ted called out.

The secretary looked around until he found his friend. "Ted!"

"What the hell is going on here?" the general bellowed. He was shaking with rage. "Arrest him!" he yelled at his commander.

"Not so fast, General," the secretary said. He calmly took a piece of paper out of his suit coat. He unfolded it and announced, "By executive order of the President of the United States, Commander in Chief, Mr. Ted Stevens, Director, DHS, and the other individuals being illegally detained under the direction of General Gilmore are hereby released."

The detainees shouted and cheered with glee.

The secretary raised his hand, asking for silence. "Furthermore, General Gilmore and his associates, both military and civilian are to be immediately placed under arrest."

Several marines emerged from the helicopter and approached the general and his commander. The general stood firm, arms folded, until several of the marines took out their pistols and pointed them at his head.

The general dropped his arms and one of the marines turned him around to place handcuffs on him.

"Let me do it!" Sue called out. "Please, please let me do it!"

The secretary laughed. He watched as the marines took the general and the commander into custody. The other soldiers under the general's command put their hands on their heads and were also escorted away.

The secretary turned to the marine standing next to him and said, "I think we can release these people." He pointed at Ted and the clones. "Please remove those cuffs."

The marine followed the instructions, and soon all were untied. Ted approached his friend and shook his hand. "Thank you, Chuck."

"Plan B," he replied. "It took us a while to get things mobilized, but it looks like we arrived just in time."

Ted nodded.

The clones, family, and friends huddled around the secretary to hear what he had to say.

"The President has already been in communication with other leaders," the secretary said, looking around at each person. "It seems the general didn't quite follow protocol. He used military connections to carry out his plans instead of following diplomatic procedures. The general has many friends here and around the world. He managed to convince those friends that you and the clones posed a credible threat to security. He showed them the email messages you all wrote, un-translated, still in your language, of course, and said the coded messages detailed an alien takeover plot."

"How could that many people believe him?" Sue asked.

"A lot of people will believe anything when it comes to terrorism," the secretary told her, "or they'll believe anything that people in power tell them. It seems the general was very convincing."

"But that's crazy," Brandy said.

"There can't be that many ignorant people in the government, can there?" Patsy asked.

"Well, there were enough people that did believe the general, or at least were intimidated by him to be able to help him."

"Then how did you stop this? How did you get people to help you?" Patsy asked.

"I had some help," he said with a smile. "Once I found the videos, I showed them to the First Lady. She remembered you all, well, the U.S. clones. She watched the videos and was moved by them, especially the one with all of you together."

The clones and friends looked among themselves and smiled with pride.

"She was outraged at what she saw and what I was able to tell her. She immediately took me to see the President. She showed him the videos and told him this had to be investigated. I told him all I knew, and he said he'd look into it. Last night, the President called me to his office. He gave me the executive order and informed me of the plan that he put in place. He told me to saddle up. And so, here I am."

"Thanks Chuck," Ted said, patting his friend on his back. "What would we do without you?"

"It was you, Ted. When you said 'Plan B', I knew you were up to something. It didn't take long to figure it out."

"I did nothing," Ted replied. "It was Brandy who did it all, she and her new friends, Eline and Aki."

Brandy blushed. "I had help. It was all of us."

"It was mostly you, though," Eline said to her.

Denise hugged Brandy and gave her a kiss. "I'm so proud of you, Brandy." she told her.

"Dee-Dee!" Suzanne called out.

Everyone laughed.

"So now what?" David asked the secretary. "What happens to the general? What happens to us? Can we go back home?"

"The general and his military associates will face a court-martial hearing. It's up to the military to decide the discipline. But I don't think we'll be calling him 'General' too much longer."

The others smiled.

"As for Mr. Wright and Mr. Mason, they'll be called before congressional hearings for violation of regulations. It's pretty clear the committee took a few too many liberties with their authority."

"What about us?" Sue asked.

"You're free to go," the secretary announced. "Any minute now, two planes will arrive to transport you all away from here. One will take the Americans back home, and the other will take our visitors to Washington where they'll meet with their ambassadors and be flown home, to their own countries. I have the President's assurance there will be no further action.

Everyone cheered and danced. It was over. They were going home.

Ted pulled the secretary aside and whispered in

his ear. The secretary listened and shrugged. He nodded at Ted and they shook hands.

"Oh," the secretary said, reaching into his coat pocket. "You might want this." He handed Ted a cell phone.

"Thanks," he told his friend.

Chapter 33 - The Happiest of Days

Two white vans pulled up to the Exchange, driven by the marines. The lead driver got out and announced, "Those of you flying to Washington, D.C., please take a seat in one of the vans."

Brandy and Eline stood next to each other. "I guess this is it," Brandy said.

"Yes it is," Eline replied. "But this is not the last time we will see each other. We will still communicate, and one day we will see each other again. I want to know how Suzanne is growing."

"Su-Su!" she called out from Denise's arms.

"And I want to see Lotta grow up, too," Brandy told Eline.

"La-La!" the other baby replied.

Aki approached Brandy and said, "I am honored to meet you." He gave her a small bow. "You change my life in many ways. The other clones and I in Japan will not be the same after meeting you."

"Thank you, Aki. And I am honored to have met you. You have changed my life also." She bowed to him.

The American clones all said goodbye to their new friends from across the oceans. They all promised to continue writing and sharing videos.

Eline gave Brandy a final hug, and took the last seat in the front of the van.

Brandy waved to Eline as the vans pulled away. She turned and hugged her mother, and then hugged her sister. "We'll see Lotta again," she told Suzanne.

"La-La," her sister replied, quietly.

The Americans quietly stood in the street and waited for the plane to take off. After a few minutes, the roar of the jet sounded as it rose and banked, heading east.

Shortly after, the vans returned to take the remaining people back home. The secretary placed his hand on Ted's shoulder and said, "The marines and I will return in the helicopter. I'm going back to Washington. When you get there, call me."

"I will, Chuck. And thanks again." Ted shook his friend's hand, but then pulled him into a hug.

Ted was the last to board the vans. When he buckled up, they drove off to the airstrip. The Secretary of the Interior smiled as the last of the detainees rode to freedom.

When everyone had climbed into the jet and found seats, Ted pulled the pilot aside and talked to him. The pilot gave him a thumbs-up response and entered the cockpit.

Ted took a seat in the front. He reclined his seat and stretched his feet out, smiling to himself.

After an hour in the air, travelling east, Denise stood and called out, "Ted, it's been a while since we took off. Why aren't we in Burbank yet? Aren't we going there first?"

Ted stood up and faced the others on the plane. "We are not going to Burbank," he announced.

"Why not?"

"We're going directly to Kansas."

"What?" Sue called out. "Why?"

Ted just stood and smiled.

Sue said, "That doesn't make sense to take us home first and then go back to California."

"Well," Ted calmly replied, "I thought that, since we were all together, we ought to celebrate."

The children and the adults buzzed with excitement. They all liked the idea.

"And..." Ted said, raising his hand to get everyone's attention. "While we're all in Kansas, we might as well have a wedding!"

The plane erupted in cheering. Ted stood in front, smiling from ear to ear.

After another hour of constant chatter from the travelers, the plane descended and landed in Abilene.

Only one van remained in the hangar, from a few days before, when they were taken away, so Ted suggested that David and Sue take the kids to open their house. Denise asked if she could ride along and take Suzanne. The baby needed rest. No one objected. Petunia volunteered to drive the van back to Abilene after dropping off the first group.

While the rest waited for Petunia to return to the airport to pick them up, Ted said to Susan, "We need to get some supplies. We need a wedding cake, and we need party supplies. Where can we get those?"

Susan gave Ted several options for stores in the area where they might find what they needed.

"Hopefully Sue won't mind if we take a few

minutes to do a little shopping," Ted told her.

"I don't think it'll be a problem," she replied with a smile.

The others stood around Ted and Susan and made a few more suggestions as to what else to buy for the party. "We might need a few hours to get all that stuff," Ted joked, realizing all that they needed to buy.

After being picked up by the van and taking a detour to go shopping, the rest of the group finally arrived at Sue's house. The adults unloaded the vans while the kids played. Sue and David directed traffic.

Soon after, a delivery van pulled up. "That's our chairs and tables," Ted said. He met the delivery men and instructed them where to set up for the party.

Ted called everyone. The adults began to assemble while Sue and David nudged the kids outside. Soon everyone was standing in the yard.

"I know this may not be the most ideal setting. And it still a little cold outside, especially for you California and Arizona folks, but I was only able to find one minister in town. He's taking the next few days off to go fishing, so unless anyone objects, I'd like to suggest we have the wedding today, right now."

Everyone cheered.

"What do you say?" Ted asked David and Sue.

"Since we're all here…" David began, hesitantly.

"Of course!" Sue finished. She turned to David and hugged him. "We're getting married!"

David smiled and hugged her in return. He kissed his bride to be.

Suddenly, Sue pulled away. "What will I wear?" she asked. "I don't have a dress!" she called out in a panic."

"Don't worry," Susan said. "I think I can loan you something. And I'm pretty sure we're about the same size," she joked. "C'mon," she told Sue, taking her hand and leading her across the street.

"What are you going to wear?" Donald asked David.

"I might have something," he replied with a grin. "Let me go see what I can find." He walked inside the house.

"Okay, everyone, we're having a wedding!" Ted announced.

Petunia returned with the minister just as David walked out of the house in his best suit. Everyone whistled at how snazzy he looked. And then Susan returned, wearing a plain blue dress. "Does everyone know their places?" she asked.

"Where's Sue?" David asked.

"It's bad luck to see the bride before the wedding," Susan replied. "Don't worry, she's ready. She'll be out as soon as the ceremony starts."

Denise asked, "Who's the Maid of Honor?"

"Sue asked for Martha," Susan said.

"But I'm not dressed for a wedding," Martha said. "I only have these dirty clothes on."

The others assured her that what she had on would be perfect.

"Sue also wants her girls to be bridesmaids," Susan announced. Kati's and Violet's faces lit up. "And of course," she added, "Karen must be one too."

"Yea!" Karen called out. "My big sister's getting married!"

"And Sue said that Brandy must be a bridesmaid, too."

Brandy blushed and smiled.

"Who's your best man?" Donald asked David.

"I think it's obvious. The boys have to be here with me."

Zachary and Tyler both pumped their fists and said, "Yesss!"

"But I need three more," David said. "We have to balance, right?" The others agreed. "Okay, Donald, Larry, and Richard, you're it."

"What about Ted?" Janet asked.

"I suggest Ted give the bride away," David told the others.

"I would be honored," Ted replied. "Thank you."

"So, are we ready?" Juliana called out. "Let's get this party started!" Everyone cheered. "I'll take Ted to get Sue. Where is she?" Juliana asked Susan.

"On the other side of David's old house," Susan replied.

"Got it." Juliana and Ted walked the distance to the old house, and then she ran back. "Okay!" she yelled. "We're ready! Come on down!"

Sue emerged from around the house and walked arm-in-arm with Ted. She wore Susan's white wedding dress.

Everyone gasped when they saw Sue. They smiled and whispered as they looked back at Sue, who was slowly walking and smiling. Tears welled up in the eyes of the women.

When they reached the wedding party, Ted took Sue's hand and gave it to David. She kissed Ted and said, "Thank you."

The minister started the ceremony and got as far as "With these rings." He looked at David and whispered, "Do you have the rings?"

David stuttered, "I... I didn't... We..."

"Oh, my bad," Ted said, walking up. He reached into his pocket and pulled out two wedding bands. "They're nothing flashy," he whispered, "but they'll do until you get some of your own liking." He handed them to David, gave him a quick nod, and quickly sat back down.

When the minister said, "You may now kiss the bride," everyone clapped and cheered. The kids jumped up and down, dancing with each other. The women wiped tears of happiness from their eyes.

Juliana stepped forward and told the newlyweds, "You two just sit here while the rest of us prepare the reception."

Susan and Denise corralled the kids while the others retrieved the food and drink from the kitchen. Donald and Larry put the beverage bottles and cans in the tub along with ice, and then laid out the plates and utensils. Petunia, Janet, and Mary brought out the food, while Martha made a pot of coffee. And Richard and Juliana carried the cake.

When all was ready, everyone helped themselves, and soon they were all sitting, settling down from the flurry of the day's happenings.

Through the quiet, Donald called out, "A toast!" Everyone raised their drinks. "To the happy couple! May your life together be the happiest of days!"

The others said, "Aw," and "Here, Here," and "Congratulations."

David and Sue stood up. David raised his drink. "Although this day wasn't exactly what we had in mind when we thought about our wedding, today has been the most memorable day of our lives. Thank you all for being here and celebrating with us. And thank you, Ted, for all that you have done for all of us over the past eighteen months. It has been the craziest year and a half of my life, I guarantee. And…" he said, looking at Sue, smiling, "I have a feeling the next few years of my life are only going to get even more crazy."

Everyone laughed, smiled, and cried.

Sue stepped forward. "I was going to tell you all before," she said, looking to each of her friends, "but then everything happened over the past few weeks, so I never got the chance. But… now I can tell you…" She blushed and then smiled. "I'm pregnant."

SUE'S VOICE

Epilogue

A red convertible sports car pulled around the corner and drove into the driveway. As he pulled up to the house, the driver turned down the volume of the music. "Yep," he said to himself, "this'll work just fine."

He got out of the car, straightened his Hawaiian print shirt, and adjusted his sunglasses. Instead of walking up to the house, he walked around the garage to the back yard.

Five children swam in the pool while a man cooked food on the barbecue grill. He refilled the drinks of two women who relaxed in lounge chairs. The two looked identical except for the length of their hair. Well, that, and the one with long hair was also pregnant.

"Ted!" the pregnant woman called to the man walking through the yard. "What in the world are you doing here?"

"Hi Sue! You look good. How do you feel?"

"Great!"

The kids in the pool saw the man pass by, and yelled, "Ted!"

"Hey kids," he said, giving them a wave of his hand. When he reached the chairs, he greeted the other woman, "Hi Susan."

"What a surprise! Hello Ted. What brings you to Enterprise?"

"Eh, I was just in the neighborhood, so I thought I'd drop in and say hello."

"Just in the neighborhood, huh?" David said. "That doesn't sound like the Ted I know. And you don't look like the Ted I know."

"I'm not the Ted you know," he replied with a smile. "I'm officially retired."

"Really?" Sue asked. "Are you serious?"

"Yep. I went back to Washington and cleaned up my messes at the department. It took me a couple months to do it. And then, last week, I said *adios*. I'm now a free man."

"So you came to see us?" Sue asked. "Why?"

"Well, I got to thinking. 'What do I want to do?' I hadn't had much time while working to give it much thought. But this past weekend, I thought it over, and the thing that came to mind was Enterprise."

"Okay!" Sue replied. "Welcome! Stay for dinner."

"Don't mind if I do. Thanks." Ted paused for a moment and looked back toward the house where he parked his car. "While I'm here," he began, looking at David, "I have a proposition." He put his hands up and shook his head. "Now, you're under no obligation. I'm not here in any official capacity. I'm just here as a friend."

"Okay…" David replied hesitantly.

"I wonder if you might consider a business transaction." He pointed his thumb behind him and continued, "You see, there's a perfectly good house over there just sitting empty. So I thought I might purchase it from its owner… if he'd agree to sell it to me."

Sue sat up in her chair with her eyes wide and a huge smile on her face. "Of course he will!"

About the Author

Andrew D. Carlson wrote the first two books in this series: *Sue's Fingerprint* and *Sue's Vision*. These are both available through Amazon.com

When he is not writing books, Andrew is a biochemist in the biotech industry.

Andrew lives in Los Angeles with his wife and son.

Follow Andrew at http://andrewdcarlson.com
on Twitter: @andrewdcarlson
on Facebook: Sue's Fingerprint

www.ingramcontent.com/pod-product-compliance
Lightning Source LLC
Chambersburg PA
CBHW070550130626
46556CB00001B/101